I0607819

LOVE LESSONS

Copyright © 2018 Susan Lute
Crazy Hair Publishing, Portland, OR

ebook ISBN: 978-0-9981029-5-5
print ISBN: 978-0-9981029-6-2

All rights reserved. Except for use in any review, the reproduction or utilization of this work in whole or in part in any form by any electronic, mechanical or other means, now known or hereinafter invented, including xerography, photocopying and recording, or in any information storage or retrieval system, is forbidden without the written permission of the publisher.

This is a work of fiction. Names, characters, places and incidents are either the product of the author's imagination or are used fictitiously, and any resemblance to actual persons, living or dead, business establishments, events or locales is entirely coincidental.

★ebook originally published 2013 in the Girls Most Like To anthology, The Girl Most Likely To Conquer New York

Love Lessons

A
Sellwood Novella
BOOK FOUR

SUSAN LUTE

This book is dedicated to Darla Luke and Ginger Kent, my co-conspirators in this lovely journey.

And to my readers Marie Edwards, Nancy Brophy, and Terri Reed. And to Wendy Warren, who gave me the tough talk when I needed it. This story is a direct result of all your support and love. Thank you, from the bottom of my heart.

ONE

S HE WANTED A MAN. AND not just any man. A Real man. One who's primary concern wasn't his social standing or the amount of money in his bank account, but rather friends and family.

Lifting her graphite pencil from the detailed graphic she was sketching, Lacey Daniels sighed heavily. Georgette could be such a royal pain in the butt. Sunlight streamed across the sketch as she drew a thought bubble around Georgette's gotta-have-the-perfect-man musings. She drew a second bubble.

And if someday a daughter came with the same color eyes as this illusive perfect man—

Pfft! Lacey snorted. There was no such thing as the perfect man. Not in her book anyway. If there was—

She drew a professor type in a rumpled, tweed suit coat and jeans, with shaggy hair and big feet. Smiling at her illustration, she returned to Georgette's demands.

He must be honest. Kind. Faithful—that's an important one. Real. Lacey crossed that out and replaced it with... *genuine. Not a man who was still a boy, but a man who'd grown into his feet, who was a grownup, and whose word meant something.*

Her doorbell peeled through the apartment. Lacey tossed her pencil on the table. Ge's list of must-haves continued to grow in her mind while she went to answer the summons.

He would cut off his right arm before he'd let his girl down. He'd stick by her through thick and thin, in sickness and in health. He laughs a lot. At himself. At life.

Ge was kidding herself if she thought that kind of man even existed, Lacey snickered as she opened the door to find her new neighbors. Beth Tyler and her ten year-old daughter, Hannah beamed at her with identical mischievous smiles lighting their faces. They'd moved in next door the previous month and she'd become instant friends with the wacky pair.

Beth's engaging laugh preceded her into the apartment. Holding out an empty measuring cup, she said, "It sounds corny, I know, but I need to borrow a cup of sugar. We can pay with cookies once they're baked."

Lacey laughed, too. How could she not? Beth and Hannah had that effect on her. "What kind of culinary student runs out of sugar?"

"The kind who feeds her neighbors."

"In that case, I have all the sugar you need." She took the measuring cup and led Beth to the kitchen.

Hannah made a bee-line for her worktable. "What are Georgette and Jack up to today?"

Georgette and her best friend Jack were the main players in Lacey's comic strip, *Love Lessons 101*. From the moment her young neighbor had made the discovery that Lacey was a cartoonist, she'd become fascinated with the stars' antics.

"We're still working that out."

Hannah giggled. "You talk like they're real people."

Lacey grinned, then shrugged. There was a lot of truth to that observation. In many ways Georgette and Jack *were* real to her. It didn't help that Ge had a mind of her own, and now that she was fast approaching thirty had decided to find her perfect guy.

Ge's talk of finding this paragon started with the invitation that came in the mail that morning. Lacey wasn't convinced in the face of Georgette's full blown panic that there were less fish in the ocean just because she'd turned thirty and was still single.

Romance queens of the Pacific Northwest for the last two years, she and Ge had hopefully managed to make the old-fashioned idea of courtship look sexy and fun for the loyal readers of *The Oregon Tribune*. Still there was no guy, perfect or otherwise, on the horizon for Ge. Maybe it *was* time to let the comic star have her way; perhaps even go on a date or two.

If *Love Lessons* gained sudden national notoriety and syndication in the process, wouldn't *that* be awesome news to share with her high school girlfriends at their upcoming turning-thirty reunion? She put that thought on pause. What she really needed was a date for the party.

Hannah picked up Lacey's doodle pad. "What's this?"

Replacing the sugar box and handing the now full measuring cup to Beth, she joined the ten-year-old, placing an arm around the girl's slight shoulders. "Georgette's list of must-haves in the perfect man."

Releasing Hannah, Lacey picked up the discarded drawing pencil, tapping the end against the fingers of her other hand. Not a single one of Ge's requirements could be laid at the feet of her own personal failure, Stephen Morse.

Okay, maybe they could, which demonstrated the hazards of hitching her wagon to such a low life and pouring her heart into a relationship that wouldn't have gotten off the ground if she hadn't been so blinded by something old, something new, something borrowed, and something blue.

"Is Georgette getting a boyfriend?" Hannah stole her pencil and proceeded to draw fat, smiling bumble bees along the outer edges of Ge's list. The girl had awesome talent.

"She wants one but I'm not sure the right guy is out there." Just because she'd crashed and burned in the happy-ever-after department didn't mean Ge had to be struck with the same bad luck.

Hannah paused in her drawing and looked up quizzically. "Are you looking for the right guy?"

Lacey patted the girl's shoulder. "Noooo. I don't have time to go on dates."

"That's what mom says." Hannah went back to her bumble bees.

"It's the truth." Beth's brows arched, an amused smirk curling her lips. "So why do you write a comic called *Love Lessons* if you don't date?"

That was the million dollar question, wasn't it? Why *Love Lessons 101* instead of *The Everyday Adventures of Georgette Posey?*

"I've been there, done that, wished I didn't have the tee shirt to prove it. And I want to help others avoid the same mistake I made; encourage them to take time to get to know each other before thinking wedding bells and honeymoons." Plus, she wanted to prove, even if only to herself, she could grow from her mistakes.

"Mission accomplished, I'd say," Beth said with a perceptive grin. She tugged on her daughter's sleeve to get Hannah's attention. "We'd better get cracking if we want to get these cookies made."

Lacey was suddenly hungry for something other than a new boyfriend. "What kind of cookies are you making?"

"M and M ones. We'll bring you some when they're done," Hannah promised as she took the sugar from her mom.

"My favorite." She ruffled Hannah's short chestnut curls. "You can bring me cookies anytime as long as you have one with me."

Beth stopped at the door. "Don't forget you promised to speak to my class on Thursday."

The younger woman was taking a *Romance Through The Ages* class as part of her college studies. At her instructor's urging, she'd asked Lacey a week ago to give a short talk on *The Lost Art Of Romance*. The lecture would be great exposure for the comic. "I haven't forgotten."

"Zane will be speaking, too."

The door snicked closed before Lacey thought to ask what subject the beloved and highly acclaimed brother, Zane Tyler, was lecturing about. Before she could block it, a tiny zip of excitement settled somewhere in the region of her belly. Now there was a man to drool over. At least according to his sister and niece.

Lacey hadn't met him, but all Beth could talk about was the older brother she'd only recently become reacquainted with when he rescued her and Hannah from a tough situation, insisting on helping them find a place to live she could afford and a part-time job so she could go back to school. Even Hannah insisted he was perfect and an awesome baby sitter—not that *she* needed a babysitter.

He sounded too good to be true. No man was that special, except perhaps her dad whose love letters to her mother were tucked in her lingerie drawer. Her mom had fallen head over heels with her dad from the very first line he'd written. Tied together with a silk ribbon saved from their wedding bouquet, the aging pages were why Lacey couldn't give up on romance or the idea that somewhere out there was a guy who matched her heart in every way.

The one time she'd taken the plunge, she'd fallen hard. At first sight. And it'd turned out to be a monumental mistake. A month later she was engaged. Another month, she'd given up the goods. The next, Stephen was gone. There was no happy-ever-after waiting in the wings. Virgin sex was all he'd wanted.

Since then she'd been on a few dates. Nothing special. And none of the guys had healed her bruised heart. It could be depressing, except it was what it was. So she was taking a break from men.

Picking up the embossed invitation from the coffee table, she ran her fingers over the glossy card. *Rosewood High. Girls Most Likely To—* She was the girl most likely to conquer New York. Hadn't happened, but it still could if *Love Lessons* went viral...and if she ever wanted to leave Portland.

She let the invitation fall back to the table. Her immediate goal was getting national syndication for Georgette and *Love Lessons*.

Putting the circling thoughts of Zane Tyler—who was, as far as she was concerned, just another guy who would turn out to be not worth his weight in gold— out of her mind, Lacey went back to her worktable and slashed a dark line through Ge's ideal man.

There was no point in looking for the perfect guy when lasting love was nowhere to be found.

Zane Tyler sat in the posh office of Alexis Karl, CEO of Phoenix, the largest maker of colognes and perfumes in the Pacific Northwest. Alexis' office overlooked the Willamette River. A confirmed bachelorette, she liked ultra-modern furnishings, edgy clothing, and men on the fast climb up the success ladder. He should know. He'd known her since their first chemistry class in college.

A brilliant biochemist, after finishing at Stanford, she'd taken over her father's ailing cologne company. It'd taken her six years to drag Phoenix into the black, but she'd done it with sheer hard work and a large dose of bullheadedness—which he admired.

And she was no fool. While she enjoyed making him uncomfortable by giving him the once-over, as long as he'd known her, Alexis had never mixed business with pleasure. So why hadn't they hooked up in the personal department? No sparks. Though he didn't believe in all that sappy romance nonsense, and given his theory about how mates are chosen, he was glad his personal scent did nothing for his friend.

When he left his last job to start his own lab and needed a buyer, Alexis was the first person he'd contacted. At the moment, she was proving his instincts had been spot on.

As an experiment, before their meeting he'd splashed on his most recent creation, a musky scent with a blend of aromatic, spicy molecules from the Far East.

Alexis' dark eyes sparkled as she leaned forward, delicate nostrils flaring. "Is that the new scent?"

Pushing her chair back, she circled her desk and leaned against the dark wood in front of him. Her nylon clad leg brushed his pant leg, mid-thigh pencil skirt showing off a long length of leg. Black hair bobbed around her ears. The look in her eyes was predatory.

Satisfied with her reaction, he eased back in the chair, laced his fingers together across his belt buckle, and tapped his thumbs in time to the beat of the victory band playing in his head. "What do you think?"

"Mmmm," she hummed. "Delicious."

His life consumed with making a success of his fledgling lab and providing security for his sister and niece, Zane wasn't looking for female companionship. Nonetheless, the attention was flattering. And the money from this sale, along with royalties from his newly released book, would go a long way toward achieving his immediate goals.

As a bonus, it would get him the foothold he needed in the industry. He'd sunk every penny he could lay his hands on into the startup of the lab. And with his impractical, self-absorbed mother enjoying a European vacation with her latest boyfriend and Beth, for the first time, willing to let him help her and Hannah, living from hand to mouth was no longer an option.

He corralled his excitement. Not that he believed in bad luck—all right, he did. He could taste success and didn't want anything unexpected to jinx things before he and Alexis had signed on the dotted line. "Let's sign the deal, then."

He didn't need another disaster like the one that had Beth, pregnant at sixteen, running as far away from home as she could get. He hadn't protected his baby sister when she needed him the most. So absorbed with his own crap, he'd been MIA when she told their mother there was a baby coming.

Nanette's first reaction had been to demand Beth give the baby up for adoption. Calculating and always on the take for a man with the biggest portfolio, their mother had been on her third marriage and didn't want the complications of an unwed daughter or the added burden of helping raise an unwanted grandchild.

Independent and stubborn, Beth had disappeared. He'd never stopped looking for his sister, but it wasn't until two months ago that she'd called from Miami asking him to come get her and her daughter. She wanted to come home.

He hadn't asked questions, just took the first flight out.

Alexis sat behind her desk and tapped manicured fingernails on a copy of his book. "I read your book. It's good."

Did she have to sound so surprised? "Thanks. I think."

"If we can make a deal with your publisher—and I'm sure we can—we'll launch the new cologne with signed copies of the book." She dragged one hand, fingers spread wide, through the air as though reading a bold headline. "Buy *Rough Diamond,* cologne for real men, and get a free, autographed copy of *The Power of Pheromones.* What do you think?"

The Power of Pheromones, his first book, detailed the research he'd undertaken, the how, where, why, and when, to prove his scientific conclusion that pheromones were the driving force behind men and women coming together in a lasting relationship. It was logical. Successful alliances were built on that first pheromone attraction, not hearts and flowers as the holiday retailers would have shoppers believe.

"Sounds great. When will the new cologne be ready to hit the market?"

"It depends on your recipe and the manufacturing

process, but maybe eight-ish weeks, longer if we want to get the marketing right. I have a meeting in ten minutes, so I'll work on a contract tomorrow."

Zane looked at his watch. It was later than he thought. "Gotta go." He shook Alexis' hand to seal the deal. "So I'll see you next week?"

She eyed him with the feral female look he remembered from their college days that meant she was looking for a date. He grinned. The new scent would take him a long way towards taking care of Beth and Hannah.

"When's the book signing?"

"This evening, but first I promised Beth I'd give a lecture to her university class. I don't want to be late."

Alexis hung onto his hand a moment longer than was necessary, making him a little uneasy. He liked their relationship just as it was. Good friends and now business partners.

With a flirtatious grin at his discomfort, she led the way to the reception area just outside her office. "Evelyn, give Mr. Tyler an appointment for next Wednesday. Make it for noon. We'll do lunch."

An amused wink had him sighing in relief. She was playing with him, not trying to start something that would be disastrous for them both. The very last thing he needed was to be distracted by a woman who would expect his entire attention.

There was room for only two ladies in his life, Beth and Hannah. He'd let his sister down once. He wasn't going to make that mistake a second time.

TWO

LACEY HAD PULLED INTO A parking spot at Portland State University when her cell started to ring. She ignored it, but the caller wouldn't quit. Finally, exasperated because she hadn't given herself enough prep time, she answered. "Hey, Fran."

"What took you so long?" Fran Halloway was her editor at *The Oregon Tribune,* and her friend. And a darned fine one at that.

"I'm running late, Fran. What's up?"

"Late for what?" Before she could answer, Fran took a quick breath and rushed on. "Forget that. This week's copy's not here. Is there a problem?"

Problem? Only Georgette being a stubborn, uncooperative hussy. "No, just having trouble with the story line. I need to iron out a few details. I'll have it to you by tomorrow afternoon at the latest."

"Cutting it close, don't you think? I need it by one to get it into the Sunday edition."

"I'll make it in time, I promise." Lacey gathered her notes with one hand.

Her editor's enthusiasm wasn't hampered in the least by Lacey's promise. In her full-speed-ahead way, Fran moved on. "Have you read *The Power of Pheromones?*"

"Haven't heard of it." Her mind cutting to the lecture

she was about to give, she pinched the cell between her ear and shoulder and grabbed her purse.

Why hadn't she changed to her bigger satchel so one bag would hold all her goodies, including her notes? One of these days her lack of organization in everything but *Love Lessons* was going to be more than a major inconvenience.

"It's a new release. The author is signing at Powell's Books on Burnside tonight at seven. You should go. You'll find it interesting." The laughter in Fran's voice raised Lacey's suspicions. "It may even help iron out those pesky details keeping you from finishing this week's comic on time."

Lacey locked her car and eyed the door into the university building where she was due to give her lecture. "Pheromones?"

"Just buy the book and read it," Fran ordered and hung up.

Pocketing her cell she hurried toward the building, trying to puzzle out Fran's cryptic call.

All of a sudden bumped from behind, her lecture notes scattered. Strong fingers circled her arm, preventing her from dropping into a squat to retrieve the jumbled mess. She muttered a curse.

"I'm so sorry," a deep male voice rumbled near her shoulder. "All my fault. Let me help you with those."

Heart thumping, she spun to face a tall, total stranger bending down to recover her papers. When he straightened, a sheepish grin curled the corners of his mouth.

Lacey couldn't help it. She stared. Something—just her heart pumping blood as it was supposed to— flipped in a slow, appreciative roll that left her a little breathless. All right, a lot breathless.

Light brown hair was cropped close around his ears.

Gray eyes circled by a band of blue held a hint of embarrassment. Dimples flirted. How cute was that?

At five-foot eight, plus heels, she rarely had to look up as she did with this guy. More than a little intrigued she was inching away for a better view when it struck her. The man was the spitting image of Georgette's ideal guy. Or at least the one she'd drawn. Now that was just plain weird.

His gaze lingered on her face. Warmth flushed her skin as he pushed the jumbled papers he'd gathered into her hands. "Here."

"Thanks." Taking the bundle, she hoped he didn't noticed how her voice squeaked.

"I'm, uh, late. For a lecture," he said, stormy eyes darkening as his gaze dropped to her lips.

Arms full of purse and disheveled papers, she made her feet move toward the building. The handsome stranger making her body snap to attention with a *hello!*, keeping pace. What in the heck was wrong with her?

There was no way she could be this attracted to a complete stranger. Attracted in a very minor way, perhaps. But not knock-her-socks-off, send up the white flag, I'm...wow, attracted. No.

Just because Georgette had decided it was time to look for love, in all the wrong places she might add, like local bars and dance clubs and on internet dating sites, love at first sight just didn't happen. At least not for her anymore. She'd learned that painful lesson with Stephen. His face flashed in her mind with that charming wink that had won her over the first time they'd met. It was a while before she figured out that split second blink was his weapon of choice when he was chasing something he wanted. And when he got whatever had caught his attention? Well, charm was put back on the shelf until he was ready to use it again.

"Me, too. I mean—I'm giving a lecture, too."

They'd reached the building. "Let me get the door."

Losing her usual glib conversation skills, Lacey could only nod. Men with old-fashioned manners were her Achilles heel because they were a dying breed. When most girls in their right minds came across such a rare beast, they snatched the guy up in a heartbeat.

There would be no snatching today. A little dazed, she ordered the surge in her pulse to slow down. "Thanks."

His crooked smile didn't help her pumping blood cool down.

Realizing she'd forgotten the room number where her date with a podium was to take place, she searched the mess of papers for the title page of her notes where she'd left the reminder.

It would be polite to ask the guy's name, wouldn't it? But when she looked up from her search, it was too late. He was gone and all that was left of her strange encounter with Ge's guy was a notable sigh of regret, which she had no time for. It was better anyway not to get distracted. She didn't have time or energy, for that matter, for a man crush.

Not too many minutes later, her strange encounter put aside for the lecture she was about to give, she faced a hall full of students. Beth waved from the front row as the instructor made the introductions. "Lacey Daniels is the author of the comic, *Love Lessons 101*. Some of you may have read it. Today she's going to talk about romance through the ages."

There was a smattering of applause, but she wasn't deterred by the apparent lack of enthusiasm. It was her favorite subject, after all. And now that she wasn't tongue tied—

At the back of the room the door opened and in walked the guy from the parking lot. Lacey's train of thought took a left, then a sharp tumble as he took a seat in the back row.

Heart sprinting, she dropped her gaze to the reorganized notes beneath her palm. She was being silly. He was just a guy she'd accidentally collided with. "It's been postulated the idea of being a romantic began in days of King Arthur's court with the first tales of the Knights of the Round Table. During the time of Lancelot, Guinevere, and chivalry, the notion of true love had a timeless quality and was sought after even more than physical love."

Lacey couldn't resist. She took a peek at Ge's guy. He was frowning. Her palms started to sweat. For a long breathless moment her words vaporized a second time. Recognizing the signs, she pulled back from the tempting precipice. She was not attracted to a complete stranger whom she knew nothing about other than his manners would make her mother proud.

The words and paragraphs of her notes emerged from the fog where they'd taken a hike and made sense again as she continued. "Today when we think about romance, what comes to mind are those small acts of courtship that are an important part of getting to know one another during the dating ritual. In our harried social environment, if dating leads to love that lasts longer than the time it takes to pick out new furniture, we consider ourselves lucky."

A student raised his hand.

"Yes?"

"Have you ever been in love, Ms. Daniels?"

Lacey hadn't planned to talk about her own experiences, but okay. She shrugged. "I thought so once. It didn't work out but I still have hope there is someone out there wanting the same things from a relationship I do. How about you?"

The student shook his head.

By the time she finished her lecture the man in the back row took another look at his watch—for what seemed the hundredth time—impatience rolling off him in waves.

Where was the nice, sexy guy who'd picked up her papers after apologizing so sweetly and then with old world charm held the door for her? Marshaling her thoughts into cool indifference, she gathered up her notes to applause from the students.

Ge's guy didn't seem to be a fan. Long strides brought him down the narrow aisle. Everything about him was so...hot...except the spark she'd taken for attraction earlier was replaced by unexpected disappointment.

He took her place at the podium with little more than a brief nod and an even briefer, "Excuse me."

Refusing to let a man she didn't know infect her fun day with his grumpiness, she descended from the stage and sat next to Beth.

"That's my brother, Zane" Beth leaned close and whispered.

Mr. Grumpy Head was her neighbor's highly acclaimed brother?

After he finished his introduction Zane Tyler adjusted the microphone for his height. "Unlike my esteemed... colleague—"

Lacey leaned back in her seat and met him stare for stare when he looked right at her all smug and condescending. The attraction that had left her breathless moments before vanished. Crossing her arms she gave him the look, a warning. *Better mind your Ps and Qs, Buddy.*

He, of course, ignored her. "—I don't subscribe to old fashioned beliefs that archaic romantic gestures will win a man the lady or bring about true love. True love? Really? No. All you need, guys and girls, is the right combination of chemicals, or if you will, the right scent to attract a mate."

Attract a mate? Had Beth's brother lost his marbles?

Putting on wire-rimmed glasses, which made him look sexier, dang it, he held up a copy of the book Fran had insisted she buy while he continued outlining his objectionable theory.

Disbelief mounting, Lacey straightened in her seat. This arrogant, pompous man couldn't possibly be Beth's sweet, caring brother? Could he? No wonder Fran wanted her to read the book. Let's see. *You could be my Prince Charming. Just give us a quick whiff. Women choose their mates by smell? I don't think so!*

"Hogwash," she muttered under her breath.

Beside her, Beth chuckled. "He told me this has been a pet project of his for a long time."

"No wonder he's not taken yet," Lacey snorted.

Everyone—at least she hoped everyone—knew romance and love made the world bright and a better place to live. Zane Tyler shouldn't be telling these impressionable kids romantic investigation was less reliable than finding someone who tickled their olfactory senses.

Despite her own failings in this area, she still believed falling in love was an exciting, spontaneous, and beautiful adventure, not a science experiment. Compatible couples were brought together by the magical dance of dating and courtship, during which they learn details about each other that proved or disproved whether they should spend the rest of their lives together. Those details couldn't be discovered by taking a passing whiff of a jumble of ingredients mingled together in a lab, for god's sake.

Insulted this...this gray-eyed throwback to the caveman didn't think women had enough sense to pick a lifetime partner with ample consideration for who or what was best for them in the long run, Lacey had only one conclusion about his ridiculous theory. "I still say hogwash."

He finished speaking midst approving hoots from the male students in the room and groans from the girls. Joining them, he wrapped his arm around Beth's shoulder and planted a brotherly smooch on her temple. Holding her in a tight hug, he leveled a smug, *so what do you have to say about that* smile at Lacey.

"Lacey, this is my idiot brother, Zane." Beth's tone held a warning to the man to behave.

Dimples showing off, his eyes sparked with self-deprecating humor. "I kind of bumped into Lacey in the parking lot."

Before she could tell Zane what she thought of his so-called theory, a recorder was shoved in her face. "Ms. Daniels. Ted Connors, book reviewer for the Portland Times. As someone who is a self-proclaimed—" He glanced at his notepad. "—Romancer, what do you think of Dr. Tyler's theory and the fact that if he is correct, not only will he kill the commercial romance business, but with the right cologne, Miss Lonely Hearts across the world could be seduced with just one sniff?"

Lacey stared at Connors, whose flashy show of teeth didn't relieve the boredom in the book reviewer's expression. He was looking for a story. She had one and had no problem giving him the scoop.

Slashing her gaze to *Dr. Tyler* she leaned toward the recorder. "I'm insulted and would encourage women everywhere to protest Dr. Tyler's crazy *theory*. Prove him wrong, ladies. Despite our human nature, a woman finding the right man and vice versa can't be managed from a test tube. It's sexy, fun, and a great adventure. Romance and love should never be reduced to the singular act of picking which fragrance to wear."

She notched her brows. "Here's a question for you, Doctor. What happens when the attracting scent wears off and you find yourself face to face with a stranger?"

Behind his glasses, Zane's gaze narrowed. Tempting lips formed into a tight, uncompromising line. "You transition from lovers to friends."

"Friends. Hmmm." Lifting her chin, she started up the aisle, then turned back to face the ill-informed man. "I have plenty of friends, Dr. Tyler. I want more in the man, if I find one, that I decide to spend the rest of my life with. Give me that formula and maybe...maybe I'll give your theory some consideration."

She marched out of the building accompanied by the niggling thought that torture wouldn't get her to admit she'd noticed Zane's spicy cologne right off.

Fran was right. Those pesky little details? They'd definitely gotten sorted out. Zane Tyler wasn't Ge's ideal man at all. He was her nemesis and it was time for romance to kick some serious science butt.

Lacey wasn't generally prone to losing her temper and took pride in the fact that she was able to rise above any situation, or had been able to until she'd managed to have a run in with stuffy, insufferable, Professor Science himself.

When she didn't know better, she'd fallen hard for Stephen, the snake. If that painful episode had taught her anything, it was that the instant attraction Zane Tyler was peddling was complete malarkey. He'd left out—perhaps on purpose...or not—stoking the flame of physical attraction with care, taking time to explore compatibility and mutual interests, and how those important steps in the dance built long-lasting mutual connection and understanding. By personal, heart-breaking experience she knew his brand of instant gratification didn't last long and rarely led the potential couple to a meaningful relationship.

The other thing she'd learned from Stephen was that she wanted something that lasted a whole lot longer than pretty fireworks. And dang it! She still believed in love, the kind that only got deeper until *death do us part*.

Lacey stalked to the kitchen for more coffee. Zane Tyler's aw-shucks boyish charm had tripped her up and had her nether regions perking up with a *you hoo*, reminding her it'd been a year since she'd dated anyone who counted charming as one of his virtues.

Stupid. Stupid. Stupid. She'd almost fallen for the Professor's shallow dribble. Fortunately for her deflated self-esteem he'd then proceeded to prove how fleeting potent attraction could be. And the reverse side of the coin, how something more meaningful made it possible for a girl to find the one guy who was interested in uncovering her inner woman.

Would Zane be interested in discovering her inner woman?

Quashing the thought as soon as it surfaced, she wished the irritating man didn't smell so delicious. It would make it easier to ignore his sad premise, which of course had no place in the dating world, unless all you really wanted was a succession of one night stands.

Bringing the coffee back to her work table, she put the finishing touches on a new episode of *Love Lessons* and signed her name with a *so there* flourish at the bottom of the last frame.

She studied the comic, finished far enough ahead of Fran's deadline to make the editor happy. In the first frame Georgette, a sassy blonde with big hair, exaggerated eye lashes, and Betty Boop boobs was introduced by her best friend, Jack, a skinny Jude Law, to Professor Science, a nerdy, wire-rimmed, bespectacled gentleman dressed in an ill-fitting suit.

Professor Science says women choose their mates by smell, Jack said with a toothy grin. If he were really man's best friend instead of Georgette's, his tale would be wagging.

Hogwash, retorts her heroine.

In the next frame Georgette offers a red rose and a book of poems to the Professor while batting her long lashes. *Romance is what makes the world go round, Professor, not a different scent for every lover.*

*But in nature, the females...*the Professor drones on in his dusty voice (Zane's voice had been just fine, in fact, better than fine, but it was her comic after all).

As the shenanigans continue, the Professor walks away smelling the rose, clutching the book to his sunken chest, red hearts floating around his head. In Georgette's bubble—*there is no question, of course women are won over by the delicate art of courting. Romance rules, not a manufactured science experiment.*

Satisfied her point was made, Lacey smiled, rolled the sketch, placing it in a mailing tube. She'd take it to Fran first thing in the morning.

Put that in your pipe and smoke it, Dr. Zane Tyler.

THREE

ZANE SIGNED HIS NAME TO the title page of his book, for...Barbara, and handed it to the middle aged woman dressed head to toe in bright orange spandex.

"Phil and I have been married for thirty-seven years. Let me tell you, he's as romantic today as the day we got married in Reno by an Elvis look-alike." She hugged the book to her ample chest and winked. "Of course it hasn't hurt that he loves the smell of orange blossoms."

Quashing an internal sigh, he nodded, too distracted to explain it happened the other way around; that it was women who were attracted by their man's scent. Men were most taken with a woman's assets. Sad, but true. Whether she realized it or not there was something about her husband's cologne that attracted Barbara to the man.

Instead, all Zane could think about was a pretty lady with brown hair streaked with sunlight and innocent whiskey-colored eyes. Their skirmish at the college podium earlier in the day after finding himself kneeling at the beauty's feet still had his heartbeat thumping. Never had he been bowled over by a simple, shy smile. One accidental bump in broad daylight and everything he'd worked so hard for wanted to take a back seat in favor of getting to know the owner of that smile better.

Couldn't happen. Lacey Daniels wasn't—he wasn't sure what she wasn't. The one thing he was sure of was that he didn't have time to be attracted in a fundamental way to long, slender legs and delicate ankles encased by Roman sandals. Okay, that was pretty sexy.

Didn't matter. The woman was a throwback to another time and an idealism left behind in the past. He didn't have time to bring her up to speed. For god's sake, she even smelled like spring flowers, which of course he'd noticed. But then she started talking about romance and how romantic machinations were the motivating factor in the mating process, earmarking her as one of those women who kept Hallmark in business.

Before her lecture took the bloom off his attraction, for a brief stunning moment he'd thought she gazed at him with surprised curiosity. The same surprised curiosity that kicked his pulse into a drumbeat of desire and left him feeling like an awkward seventeen year-old. At least until he'd taken a seat in the back of the lecture hall.

He'd bet what little savings he had Lacey Daniels' heart ruled her head, which put her in the too sentimental category. Like his mother. The exact opposite of the practical, grounded women he dated on the rare occasions when he needed to get out of his lab.

What kind of job was that, drawing a cartoon called *Love Lessons 101?* And who on the whole planet took life altering advice from a cartoon character?

His mother, that's who. Nanette Wilton, remarried for the fourth time only three months ago, had spent so much time during his childhood looking for romance and the perfect man, more often than not she'd leave him and Beth to their own devices. And it was because of ideas like the romantic valentines, hearts, and flowers Daniels was peddling that his mother lost sight of the fact that her primary responsibility was to provide a loving, stable home life for her son and daughter.

Zane snorted and signed a book, for...Dan, a twenty-something guy who was a Ron Weasley of Harry Potter fame lookalike wearing dark-framed glasses that might have been transported straight from an earlier decade. The dude also carried a box of chocolates, presumably for the girl he wanted to impress. Clearly he needed *The Power of Pheromones* to set him straight.

The ink in his pen faded to nothing. Zane tossed it down and picked up another.

No matter what Lacey Daniels said, the facts of science were irrefutable. Romance was a fanciful illusion, a waste of good time, energy, and money better spent taking care of more important responsibilities.

While her wistful smile and sweet beauty had for a mind-spinning moment knocked him out of the strict confines of a very well organized life, for that blissful second he could have been his mother, willing to toss aside everything he'd worked for in pursuit of one unexpected lady.

Thank god he'd found out in time she wasn't his kind of woman, letting his brief infatuation go the way of the dodo bird.

"Are you starting a fan club?"

Man, he hoped so. Zane shook off his brooding thoughts and looked up to find Beth and Hannah standing next in line. His sister and niece were the only girls he wanted messing up his life. At least until Beth finished culinary school, or they didn't need him anymore. Truthfully, he hoped they would always need and want him involved in their lives.

There was no room for anyone else. Especially not a confusing woman so fixated on romance and all of its attending paraphernalia.

He rose, bumping his leg on the table, to give them hugs. "Thanks for coming. As for the fan club, I wish."

Wiggling out of his embrace, Hannah pointed to the bookstore's large store-front window and the three young women outside trekking back and forth carrying signs. "They seem annoyed."

As they came back, he could read the placards. *Romance makes the world go round. We do not choose our mates by smell! Romance wins over pheromones.* And the women weren't alone. Connors, that pain-in-the-ass book reviewer from the university walked with the picketers, his recorder extended as he asked questions.

"What the heck? Who are they?" Frustration crawled up his neck. "I think I recognize them. Are those girls from your class, Beth? I'll bet Lacey Daniels put them up to this."

"I don't think so, Zane." Beth grabbed his arm holding him in place instead of letting him head for the door as he intended. "We just left Lace. She's home working."

His sister had forged a strong friendship with 'Lace'. He'd heard a lot about Beth's neighbor before meeting the lady at the college. For that friendship, and that alone, he was grateful to the misinformed woman.

"Honest." Beth raised her hand. "I swear."

He remembered the challenge Lacey had tossed out to Connors before ending their earlier confrontation. *I'm insulted and would encourage women everywhere to protest Dr. Tyler's berserk theory. Prove him wrong, ladies.*

He hadn't thought much about it at the time. That

had been a mistake. While Lacey Daniels might not be there taking part in the protest mounting outside the bookstore, he was convinced she'd authored the spirit of the gathering with her parting words.

Unfortunately it was clear there was nothing he could do about the dissenting voices. If he confronted the protesters, he would give credence to their erroneous ideas and more fuel for Connors next article.

The best thing for his mission to take care of his sister and niece was to ignore the noise and get back to signing books. There wasn't a long line of folks waiting, but there was a line.

It was the next evening—after very little sleep the night before and a long day spent in the lab trying some variations on his most recent concoction—that he made the call he'd put off all day.

He couldn't get Lacey Daniels off his mind and that, in and of itself, irritated the heck out of him. The phone rang. When he was about to disconnect, she answered with a husky, "Hello?"

"Lacey? Zane Tyler here."

There was rustling in the background. Had he caught her at an inconvenient time? He glanced at the clock on the microwave as he waited for coffee to brew in the maker. Eight-twenty-four.

The husky note in her voice turned wary. "What can I do for you Mr. Tyler?"

"My friends call me Zane," More rustling. Was she in bed? He cleared his throat. "I...um...some of the students from the university were protesting at my book signing yesterday. I think they took your words too much to heart."

A surprised laugh reached him across the phone connection. "Well, first we're not friends and second, what do you want? A retraction?"

"That would be very helpful." He was surprised she was the first one to suggest it, but happy he didn't have to argue over her part in his current dilemma, or the solution he figured was due.

"Sorry." She sounded way too cheerful. "Not going to happen, Professor."

A sudden suspicion took shape in his mind. "You're not putting our disagreement in your comic strip, are you?"

"It makes for interesting copy, don't you think?"

Zane bit back a snort. He did not need this complication. "How about meeting me for a drink so we can talk?"

"Now?"

"I'll meet you anywhere you want in thirty minutes."

"Can't. It's been a long day and I'm already in bed."

Zane's libido sprang to attention with a mind-numbing shout as he envisioned golden-brown hair spread across a pillow, a slow seductive smile blooming across her cupid face.

Wait a minute, he ordered the body acting like an adolescent chump responding to his first hard crush. "I've offended you. One drink and a chance to clear this mess...misunderstanding up. That's all I'm asking."

"That's the first right thing you've said. Romance and finding love, it can be messy. Goodnight, Professor."

The phone clicked in his ear. *Professor?* She'd given him a nickname? That couldn't be good.

Sunday morning, with the *Oregon Tribune* spread

out before him, Zane hunched over his kitchen table. Lacey Daniel's comic was clever, if over the top. He still couldn't believe she'd splashed their personal conflict across the funny page of the most frequently read newspaper in Oregon. He shouldn't be surprised. After their phone call, he'd been expecting something like what he was reading. He'd just hoped she was pulling his leg.

Disgusted he'd let things get this far out of control, he reread the comic. There was no doubt about it. He'd somehow lit a fire under the pretty lady. What he hadn't expected was admiration at her sass and the spirited dialogue.

He frowned at the hearts floating around Professor Science's pointed head. Lacey's caricature bore a striking resemblance to the image he faced in the bathroom mirror every morning. The gangling, bespectacled Professor was definitely meant to be him, which made it more imperative than ever he speak to her about making public sport of a man's thoroughly researched conclusions.

More maddening than the look alike caricature, she hadn't given him a chance to ply her with reason before taking their different opinions public. Her unpredictability could put a serious dent in his business plans for the scents he was developing. Maybe if he explained how important the contract with Alexis and Phoenix was—

Why did he let Lacey's sweet smile, her unfettered directness, and the recurring image of her wearing a close-fitting tank and shorts to bed interrupt his concentration? Though he got the attraction, it was baffling. He had no time at this critical juncture for any kind of distraction, especially the *he couldn't wait to kiss the hot lady* kind.

And while he might, with enough determination, be able to ignore her spoof on his hypothesis on the off chance the caricature of his work would die a natural death if left alone, Ted Connor's book review was harder to dismiss.

Zane Tyler's first book is an interesting exposé on the mating habits of the human species. His claim that women choose their mates by smell backed by tedious documented research, while it appears well thought out, has too many facts for entertainment value. In addition, Lacey Daniels, cartoonist and author of the Love Lessons 101 *Sunday comic, claims Tyler's analysis is an insult to all women everywhere.*

Blah, blah, blah. Damn, the man couldn't have been more brutal. If the review and growing protests affected book sales, everything he'd been working so hard for would come crashing at his feet.

Zane went for more coffee and then stayed there staring out the window, but not seeing the people and cars below. What with working long lab hours to have the samples to show Alexis and the additional book signings arranged by his publisher—signings attended by a growing number of protesting women—he hadn't had a single moment to spend with Beth and Hannah.

That was the worst of the fallout from the trouble that began with a simple university lecture. And it was the one thing he had to fix as soon as possible. Reaching for the cell he had charging on the counter, instead of finding his sister's number, he called Lacey and got her message.

The sound of her leave-a-message greeting, full of an appealing optimism he hadn't encountered in, all right, forever, almost derailed his practical, take the most direct approach to put an end to their ill-advised conflict. Leaving a brief message he hoped she'd take him up on his offer of a meal in exchange for working out their current difficulty.

Beth and Hannah's future was on the line. Perhaps Daniels would agree his science was indisputable if she read his research and let him explain in more depth than he had at the university. One thing he knew, the sooner this hiccup was behind him the better it would be for everyone, especially Beth and Hannah.

By Wednesday, he still hadn't heard from Lacey despite leaving several more messages. It was stupid to be disappointed, but as the day progressed, her silence was the least of his troubles.

He wasn't selling books at his book signings. It appeared he couldn't even give them away. The number of picketing women was growing. They happily gave him roses and chocolates, but didn't buy books. The most disconcerting was the call from his editor that morning hinting sales were tanking.

Ted Connors, who'd taken to showing up whenever he was signing, had a byline in today's edition of the Portland Times titled *The Battle Between Romance and Science Heats Up.*

His disagreement with Lacey Daniels wasn't dying the quiet death he'd been anticipating. It left him with one option. Somehow he had to find a way to run into the lady. Again. Too bad kidnapping, even for just an hour, was illegal.

When his cell rang, he grabbed it, hoping the caller was the illusive woman not answering his messages. His luck wasn't that good.

"Hey brother." Beth's cheerful greeting was a blessing given what else was going on.

Needing the good cheer, Zane took his coffee to

the table and closed the newspaper so he didn't have to look at Lacey's diabolical work. "Hey yourself, brat. What's up?"

"Just confirming our trip to the Art Museum on Sunday."

He could hear Hannah singing in the background and couldn't stop a smile from spreading across his face. Taking a deep breath, he leaned back in his chair. This was why he worked so hard. It was all for his sister and niece. "Got you on my calendar."

"You work too hard, Zane," Beth chided, lifting his spirits even more. It'd been a long time since anyone cared about his obsessed work habits.

It took a lot of work to take care of a family, not that Beth let him help much. "Yeah, well. What can I say? I love my work."

"Listen, Hannah and I have been talking."

He laughed. "Uh oh"

"We think it's time you got out of your lab and went on a date."

He loved his sister, but she was the first one to tell him to back off if he became a helicopter in his efforts to give her the kind of life she hadn't had since she ran away at sixteen. Eleven hard years, from the sounds of it, had passed before she'd gotten in touch with him again. Though he didn't need dating advice, he didn't want to send her into hiding either.

"You do? That's the kettle calling the pot black, isn't it?"

"I have Hannah to think about."

And I have you and Hannah to think about.

"You on the other hand are free as a bird. You don't want to end up a lonely, bitter old man, do you?"

"Haven't got the time, remember?"

Once Beth had her mind set on something—
"We know a girl, who shall remain nameless for the
moment, who would be perfect for you if you'd give
her a chance."

The elusive Lacey Daniels popped into his mind, sun
sparkling in her dark hair, flowing skirt molding to
long legs that made a man swallow his gum, her flowery scent tripping him up as it floated on a breeze.

He scowled. "I can schedule my own dates, thank
you very much, Baby Sis."

"So says the man who bribed his niece into asking
that nameless girl to go to the museum with us."

He didn't respond to his sister's dig, hoping Beth
would let it go. But, no.

"You don't *schedule* dates, lug head," she snickered.
"You make a plan, figure out what tickles the lady's
fancy, then approach her with an invitation she can't
turn down."

Zane reared back from his cell and held it at arm's
length before bringing it back to his ear. "Forget it, kid.
So, Sunday, right? One o'clock?"

Her dramatic, heavy sigh reminded him how grateful
he was to hear even that much from the sister who
took up most of his heart. "Fine, see you then."

"Give that niece of mine a big hug."

"Absolutely." Beth's voice went gooey around the
edges. There was no one his sister loved more than her
daughter.

Determined to get a certain cartoonist out of his
mind, he pushed the tempting image of liquid,
topaz-colored eyes aside.

Two hours later, Zane was sitting at a table in Elle's,
waiting for Alexis to arrive with the contract she'd
promised. When she entered the swank, boutique

restaurant wearing a tight business number and an even tighter expression, an alarm blared in his head.

He helped her get seated, hoping like the dickens he was wrong. If she'd changed her mind there was no benefit in dragging the embarrassing ordeal out. He got right to the point. "You don't look happy. Is there a problem?"

She ordered iced tea from the hovering waiter before scooting the newspapers she'd carried in under her arm across the table. One was opened to Ted Connor's article, the other Lacey Daniel's comic strip. "Most days I don't put much stock in what the media prints but I'm concerned about the recent negative attention you've been getting from the press."

Damn. She was serious. He knew what Phoenix meant to Alexis; how hard she'd worked to bring the company back from the brink of disaster. But if she wouldn't take a chance on him, and this deal fell through, his opportunity to do business with the hottest perfume company in town was going to fail before it even got off the ground floor.

He flicked the papers. "This is just a flash in the pan." He hoped.

"Uh huh. How are your book sales going?"

He couldn't lie. Not even stretch the truth a little. "The book was only released two weeks ago."

"Just what I thought. Not doing so good." Alexis took a sip of water, her assessing gaze steady on his face.

"I wouldn't say sales are terrible." Well, he wouldn't. "The book's just starting out slow."

He would NOT panic. Too much depended on how he handled the situation.

"Don't let a crazy cartoon and book critic get in the

way of our doing business together. Next week there will be a new headline and all this nonsense will be forgotten. Please give me a chance to prove we've got a money making product here."

Silence stretched out between them while Alexis considered his request.

"Okay. We'll put the contract on the back burner for now. But Zane, I won't risk Phoenix by sinking a lot of capital into a product that has problems even before we go to production." She reached for his hand. "Not even for a good friend. Bad press isn't always good press. Somehow you have to convince Lacey Daniels and this Ted Connors to change their minds; reverse their messaging and get them on board. Our largest customer base is women. I can't chance a backlash that would threaten the rest of Phoenix's merchandise."

She couldn't—?

Alexis wasn't the only one who's future was on the line.

FOUR

L ACEY SAT AT A CORNER table of Elle's trying
to keep her eyes on anything but Zane Tyler and
the dark-haired, ultra-chic woman who'd joined him
at his table. She couldn't help staring. They were like a
flashing neon sign, a power couple; movers and shakers
who knew what they wanted and were reaching for the
moon. Focused on the lady, Zane pulled out her chair.

Lucky girl.

It took a full blown minute before she realized the
two wistful words had taken root, bringing with them
an absurd longing.

*Lacey Daniels, don't you dare. Step back from the crazy
dude who believes in smells and animal instincts instead of
falling in love. Just because he looked at you with a challenge
in those gray-blue eyes and possibly saw the real you, you're
not the one he's offering a chair.*

At the tart jab, she stared at her glass of water. The
only argument she had in her defense, for a man who
believed in science, Zane had the manners of a man
who enjoyed romancing a woman the old-fashioned
way.

"Lacey. You're not listening!"

"Sorry. I'm a little distracted." Best not to tell Fran
who was doing the distracting.

Smiling broadly, Fran leaned forward on her elbows. "Readers love today's online edition of *Love Lessons*. Response is going through the roof. It was a good idea to add a mid-week edition. Coupled with the Sunday comic, I think we've got a winner."

Lacey's success meter started to ping. If Fran liked the latest twist in the *Romance Beats Science* battle, she was going to love Sunday's comic.

Handing over the mailing tube she'd brought, she said, "The good news is there's more. I finished the next two episodes this morning."

Fran grabbed the mailer. "If these are as good as the first two, I can promise—I'm using the p word here—national syndication. Rare as that is these days, you have a good shot at it."

Zane Tyler might not like that, but she was pretty sure he wasn't even reading *Love Lessons* and Georgette's advice for adventurous romantics. Did it matter if he objected?

She stole another quick look at the frowning man across the room.

"Maybe you could have Georgette make a list of attributes for the man she's looking to find. Then, over the next installments take readers with her on the search," Fran said.

Zane's date reached across the table to hold hands. Lacey gulped water to stop the churning in her stomach.

"And wouldn't it be the perfect surprise if the Professor turned out to be that guy?"

Lacey jerked back to the conversation with Fran, almost tipping over her water glass as she carefully put it back on the table. "There's no way the Professor is Georgette's ideal man. He doesn't have a single romantic bone in his body."

Fran grinned. "That's what makes it so yummy...and surprising."

How in the world was she supposed to respond to that idea? Yummy? Like the chocolate volcano cake being gobbled down at the neighboring table?

At her silence, Fran shrugged and patted the tube. "Okay. It was just a thought. Send me the sequels as soon as you can. In the meantime, I'm looking forward to discovering what's hidden in here. Have you talked to Zane Tyler since your encounter at the university?"

Inwardly, Lacey groaned. The one topic she'd hoped to avoid.

She'd told Fran everything when she dropped off the first episode of *Romance Beats Science*. Keeping her gaze on the spaghetti she pushed around her plate and away from the guy who'd sparked a pendulum of reactions the first time they'd met, first lust, then complete disbelief, she figured it was better not to tell her editor she'd been ignoring Zane's messages or that her nemesis was at that very minute having a meal across the room behind Fran's back.

"No."

"Hmmm—" was Fran's only response.

Maybe she *should* consider returning his call. If Fran's promise of national syndication materialized, she would owe him one. A thank you note and tickets to a local play wouldn't be out of line and an appropriate response for the boost to her career, right? He could take his girl. The concession had her wondering...what scent was he wearing for his lunch date?

Lacey shook her head. It didn't matter. Thanks to Zane and their opposing points of view, she was on the brink of seeing her most cherished dream come true.

Back at her apartment Lacey searched her music until she found Madonna, made a cup of chamomile tea—boy did she need it—then took the cup with her to the bathroom where she'd already lit candles and filled her claw foot bathtub with warm water. The antique tub was the primary reason she'd picked this particular condo, and because the charming home was located on a semi-quiet street on the edge of the Sellwood district of Portland. Picturesque, tall windows overlooking a family park were an added bonus. From her desk she could watch families play and quite frankly, their happiness had her green with envy, which was very non-productive since her career held center stage for the time being.

As she poured bubble bath into the steaming water, an image of Zane Tyler gazing at her while he'd gathered her scattered papers—as if he'd discovered something new that fascinated him—rose with the steam. Splashing the water to dispel the tempting picture, she had to admit that while the man might have the wrong idea about romance, he was not hard on the eyes.

And of course it would be better than nice to get to know the man behind the crazy pheromone idea, the Zane who opened doors for a girl and whose eyes twinkled with humor, given their current stalemate, it was unlikely they'd have all that much in common. She'd dodged a bullet where he was concerned when she'd taken a front row seat and heard his crazy idea so early in the game.

Piling her hair on top of her head and securing the twist with chopsticks, she stripped and sank into the bath with a grateful sigh. Closing her eyes, she let the bubbles rise to her chin.

What would Zane think if he discovered she was a bit of a fraud? Because the truth was, girls who talked the talk should walk the walk and she couldn't. Since breaking up with Stephen—had it been three years?—she hadn't made a concerted effort to get back in the dating game.

Online dating, where safety in distance and time saved going on date after date that didn't work out, had some merit, but every time she looked at an online site, all she could think about was how she'd been fooled once. In the anonymity of the internet guys could type in whatever they wanted when they weren't sitting across the table where she was able to judge the truth of their words by the expression on their faces. Not that she was good at that either.

She didn't want to play the fool again. And the truth was, her parents had set the bar so high, she didn't want to disappoint them by making the mistake of marrying a guy who couldn't stay the course. In self-preservation she'd abandoned the dating scene and created Georgette and Frank to speak to other trusting souls like herself.

So, why couldn't she forget the pheromone theorist? Why couldn't she walk away and pretend she'd never heard his crazy idea? Maybe if she tried objectivity; gave him the benefit of the doubt; found some plausible space where his pheromone thing might make sense.

Nope. No matter how hard she tried, she couldn't accept a girl's sense of smell was the *thing* standing between her and a happy life with that special guy. As Fran's words at lunch about the Professor turning out to be Georgette's ideal man came back to haunt her, a part of her—a very minuscule, irrational part, she qualified—was sorry Zane Tyler wasn't her guy.

Emerging from the bath and wrapping herself in the rose-covered robe hanging on the back of the bathroom door, she found the gilded invitation where she'd left it on her worktable. In high school *the girls most likely to...* had made a pact to meet and celebrate their successes the year of their thirtieth birthdays. What did "the girl most likely to conquer New York" have to show for herself at their upcoming Turning-Thirty Reunion?

Tapping the parchment envelope against her fingers, Lacey snorted. Not a husband or young family that played together in the park across the street, that was for sure. But there was *Love Lessons* and the national syndication dangling just beyond her fingertips. If it happened that romance beat out pheromones in the upcoming week or two, finding the perfect man could wait for next reunion.

The bread maker beeped. Leaving the invitation, she dumped warm, fresh bread from the internal pan, savoring the smell. It smelled almost as good as Zane.

Enough of that, now. How the man smelled didn't matter. And he would soon be history, if things went the way she envisioned.

The doorbell interrupted the reminder to stay on task. Hoping it was Beth after more sugar, she went to answer the summons. The last cookies Hannah had brought over hadn't lasted the day. Maybe she could negotiate a trade. Freshly baked bread for more of the yummy snacks.

Eager to get her mind off her neighbor's pesky brother, she checked the peep hole to make sure it was Beth before she willy-nilly invited a stranger into her home. Zane Tyler rang her bell again. Talk about yummy.

Stop that! Lacey glanced down at her robe. It covered enough of everything, including her ankles.

She'd barely inched the door open when he pressed his hand against the wood, demanding, "We need to talk."

His tone wasn't happy. Well, guess what. Neither was she. "I'm busy."

The furrow between his brows deepened as his gaze flicked across her face. Leaning against the door frame, apparently with nothing better to do than hang around until she invited him inside, he said. "Take a break. It's important that we work out our differences."

Not going to happen, dude. Lacey's skin prickled with a sudden hot flush she hoped the man staring at her didn't notice. In fact, she felt a little faint. Clearing her throat she croaked out, "Got a deadline. You've written a book. You know how important a deadline is. Anyway, I'm not dressed to receive guests—"

She clamped her mouth shut, stopping the inane flow of words. What was wrong with her? Zane Tyler was a full-of-himself, stuffy science-guy. His gaze shifted downward. She crossed her arms over her chest. The robe didn't reveal anything critical, but the silky material hugged in strategic places, which his lingering gaze seemed to find without too much trouble.

Ge's list of the perfect guy flashed before her eyes, exposed where she'd left it on her desk. Panic replaced her flush. Zane couldn't see her doodling from the doorway, but she didn't need him getting close enough to read more into the list than was there—a little brainstorming in the form of scribbles as she figured out what Georgette wanted and why. She blocked his view.

"So, what do you want to talk about?" she asked, her tone suggesting she was the innocent one in their debate and had no clue why he was standing on her doorstep.

A dark brow shot up as the light of battle came into his stormy eyes. "For starters, a retraction would be nice, or whatever it is you cartoon writer-types do to apologize and say you're wrong to hundreds of readers."

She almost laughed. He was so cute. Even when he scowled and she was the recipient of his bad humor. "I haven't said anything that wasn't true." She pointed at her watch. "It's getting late and I still have some of that *cartoon writing* to do."

Leaning into her personal space, he sniffed. "Is that fresh baked bread?"

He was too close. Lacey caught herself before she smelled him in return. Still the hint of spice and coffee and showered man held her captive. An excited shiver danced a two-step down her spine. "Maybe."

"Mmm, smells delicious. I love homemade bread. Make it all the time." She didn't trust the sudden challenge that came into his eyes. "You could offer a starving man a slice smothered in butter and jam."

Her pulse thumped. She stepped back, prepared to close the door in his handsome face. "I could, but I don't share my homemade bread with just anyone, and not with someone I don't like all that much."

She fought the truth, because she did like him a little. What wasn't there to like about a guy who took such good care of his sister and niece?

"I'm not a bad guy. We just started off on the wrong foot." Aiming an unrepentant smile at her, he maneuvered said foot across the threshold, blocking the door. "You'd like me better if we could get this little misunderstanding between us resolved. There's a lot at stake."

"Yes, there is, which is why knowing you better will not change my mind about how important romance and the odd notion of a couple spending time together is for finding lifetime compatibility."

"I was kind of hoping we wouldn't have this conversation in the hallway," he pushed back. "But have you seen the divorce rate?"

Lacey put her hands on her hips before she realized the action caused her robe to gape and Zane's gaze to drop from her face. She crossed her arms again. "Those statistics prove my point. Couples today don't take time to find out if they're a good fit."

"I don't disagree with that, but I brought my book for you to read so you could see all the research that went into my conclusion—" He held out a copy of *The Power of Pheromones*.

She shook her head and reached to close the door.

His hands flew up in surrender. "Okay. I can't make you read it."

"Obviously." Standing behind the door where he couldn't see a clothing malfunction if there was one, she perched a hand on her hip. She wasn't about to tell the persistent man she already had a copy of his book, though she hadn't read it yet. Books delivered to her door were the best.

"Okay. Well. Good-bye." He turned in the direction of Beth's condo with a determined look, tossing over his shoulder, "We still need to talk."

Lacey didn't think so, but Zane was right. There was no point in arguing the matter in the hallway. "Good-bye."

Two days later Lacey, wondering who was having the last laugh, sat in a mocked up sitting room complete with a fireplace and bookshelves lining two of the fake walls. Fran had used her magic to pull some strings with the producer of the morning show, *Rise and Shine City of Roses*. Her disagreement with Tyler was about to go public on local television.

On her arrival she was informed the man who would help her reach national syndication was already there, backstage. She'd bet a ton of money a live broadcast wasn't what Zane had in mind when he'd thrown over his shoulder, *we still need to talk,* before going to visit his sister.

He'd looked so delicious, lounging in her doorway, salivating over the fresh bread cooling on her counter. The way he'd looked at her had so temped her to come out of her self-imposed bubble. Okay, it was true, standing there in just her robe had a lot to do with the thorough way he'd breathed her in. She was still warm from imagining what might have happened if she'd thrown caution to the wind and invited him into her private space. The fleeting visuals left her more than a little breathless.

How in the world had things escalated so quickly? Fran. The woman could realign the sun when she put her mind to it. And now she and Zane *were* going to have that talk. *In front of a live audience and a million viewers.*

Forcing herself to take a calming breath, she repeated the words that had become her mantra over the last few days. Zane Tyler was not that special. She was strong.

She could keep her distance from the misguided man if she wanted, which she did.

The audience quieted as the host of the show, Valerie Simons, began her opening volley. "Welcome to *Rise and Shine*, my friends. And please help me welcome an exciting guest to today's show." There was a ripple of applause. "Lacey Daniels is the author of the Sunday comic *Love Lessons 101*."

Valerie turned to face Lacey, a cagey smile lighting her face. "To get started, why don't you tell our audience a little bit about yourself, Lacey."

Lacey didn't trust that smile, but Fran had insisted exposure on the morning show in a face to face chat with Zane would sell a lot of newspapers and drive a lot of traffic to *The Oregon Tribune's* website. And if they were lucky, *Love Lessons* would go viral on social media.

Lacey wasn't sure about that, but crossed her fingers anyway. How did she tell Portlanders, and maybe more than those early rising viewers, enough about herself to make them curious, but not enough to appear like a fumbling bimbo—so to speak—in front of Tyler who was listening in on the conversation? "Well, I grew up in California and moved to Rosewood when I was a freshman in high school. I like Voodoo doughnuts, the occasional margarita, and a walk in the park."

"For our viewers who don't know the area, Rosewood is a little town close to Portland, best known for its murals and local brewing company."

Not trusting the calculating glint Valerie cast her direction, Lacey sipped from the glass of water at her elbow.

"I understand you're single?"

"I am. Haven't found the right guy yet." Lacey tried

not to think about Zane, but failed. How dumb was that?

"The good ones are super-hard to find." Valerie nodded as if they were best girlfriends sharing secrets in a cozy sports bar. She included the audience in a sweeping glance before winking at the crowd, making Lacey's nerves climb to the next level. "So you have an active dating life?"

"I wouldn't say that," Lacey returned, hoping she wasn't admitting to being something of a fraud on live television.

"Tell us about your little comic then. The main characters are Georgette and Frank?"

Lacey smiled at the audience. If she blew this chance to gain new fans for *Love Lessons* Fran would kill her. "That's right. Georgette and Frank are best friends." Warming up to her favorite subject, she relaxed and forgot that whatever Valerie had up her sleeve made her nervous, almost as much as Zane hovering backstage. "Jack is the shy one and has a hard time getting dates, so Georgette gives him advice on how to romance the ladies."

"How did you come up with the idea for *Love Lessons 101*?"

Valerie's question—as if she really cared—brought Lacey back to reality where she was sitting on a studio stage determined to sell the current love of her life. She gave a little laugh to keep up the pretense she was dishing to her best friend and not wishing she was anywhere else; even having a debate in front of a classroom of students with the obnoxious Professor about the merits of romance versus science. "Well, my boyfriend had broken up with me and the next guy I dated...let's just say he didn't inspire me to try a second date."

"Which segues nicely into the introduction of our next guest." Valerie's tinkling laugh rang Lacey's danger-danger bell. "Please welcome our next guest. Zane Tyler is a biochemist and author of the new book, *The Power of Pheromones*."

Here we go. Lacey forced a polite smile on her face as Zane strolled onto the stage oozing self-assured man on a mission. This man was nothing like the Professor who'd provoked her with his lecture at the college. *Her* mission to remain unimpressed slipped, her pulse skipping a beat or two. Sexy in a well cut, black suit showing off the width of his shoulders and an athletic physique that had to make all the women in the audience swoon, all but robbed her of the determination to keep her distance. A stern reminder that he was not the most delicious chocolate bar on the shelf almost—almost—went unnoticed by her inner bad girl.

The confidence mirrored in clear gray eyes as they lingered on her painted toes before transferring to their host left Lacey catching her breath, dang it. Bombarded with enough temptation to distract her from her ultimate finish line, she tried hard to focus on why she was on stage with a morning show host who would do anything for ratings—she'd watched several episodes as soon as Fran had told her this gig was a go—and the man who stood between her and the future she wanted for Georgette and Frank.

Waiting until the Professor took his seat, Valerie practically purred, the sound scraping like jagged nails down Lacey's back. "Tell us a little about yourself, Zane."

It was none of *her* business if Valerie, the barracuda, had the hots for Beth's brother.

"I'm chief cook and bottle washer at a lab where I spend most of my days creating scents for colognes and perfumes. No pets. No kids."

"The perfect bachelor." Valerie crossed nylon-clad legs, the move inching up her dress to reveal more. "Is there a girlfriend?"

Lacey glanced at Zane to see if he'd noticed, but to his credit his gaze never left their host's face.

"I'm not dating anyone," he said, sending Lacey a speculative glance.

Heat mounting her chest and neck, she looked down to study the floral design on her water-green tunic. Why was Zane Tyler the one who got her motor revving?

"In *The Power of Pheromones*," Valerie picked up Zane's book, holding it up for the audience. "You claim that women choose their mates by smell. Can you elaborate?"

Lacey sat back in her chair, not sure she could watch the Professor fall flat on his face on public television.

"According to my research, pheromones are a natural phenomenon that occurs in many species, including humans."

Lacey shook her head, despite the fact that the subtle scent coming off the man reminded her of Multnomah Falls in the summer. His smell wasn't the only attraction. Though she wouldn't say so out loud, there were many other things that made Zane Tyler memorable. Like how genuinely he believed his foolish theory; how determined he pressed forward even though not everyone—her—ascribed to his opinion; and how he honestly thought there was nothing wrong with his unpalatable idea.

"Studies demonstrate women choose their mates by

coming in contact with the scent of compatible males. Imagine how easy dating would be if all a woman had to do was discern the smell of a male most attractive to her, rather than wade through the so-called romantic game playing that camouflages the dating scene."

Lacey refrained from jumping out of her seat, limiting her reaction to an unladylike snort instead. Didn't the man know it was the other way around? Instant attraction was the camouflage, not dating to get to know your guy better.

Valerie's expression took on a shrewd look dripping with excitement. "You don't agree, Lacey?"

FIVE

ZANE FELT A SHARP JOLT at Lacey's soft snort.
So, it was coming down to a battle of wills. He couldn't say he was unhappy to pit his ideas against the pretty lady's. It wasn't often he met a woman who could take his mind off the work going on in his lab. Lacey Daniels had managed to do exactly that.

It was bizarre, this fascination with his sister's neighbor. He had to be careful. Granting Lacey a foothold into his world, with her old-fashioned ideas about something as simple as picking a lifetime partner—well it was ludicrous if he wanted to stick to the plan and preserve his independent bachelorhood and financial stability.

As a kid he'd watched his mom jump from one man to another looking for romance. She'd claim to find the perfect guy, uproot him and Beth from school and the friends they'd managed to make, and move them all to be with the new 'love' of her life. When the so-called romance ran cold, the search for something that didn't exist started all over again.

Romance. Hearts and flowers moments. All of it was an illusion. He'd prove it and finish up this ridiculous quarrel he'd gotten himself into.

The seating onstage was arranged in a half-moon,

three comfortable looking chairs separated by small tables with glasses of water and copies of his book standing so the audience could see the cover. He had a clear view of Valerie. Ms. Daniels sat between them.

Despite his best efforts not to notice, the cartoon lady, in her flowery dress and roman sandals that showed off delicate ankles and painted toes, made him think of spring and the first cherry blossoms. What was it about a woman's toes painted in the brightest shade of red imaginable that inspired his imagination? It wasn't like he was an inexperienced eighteen-year-old and in college surrounded by the unlimited bounty the feminine world had to offer.

Focusing on Valerie, he cleared his throat and glanced at the audience to gauge their reaction to the reasonable facts he was attempting to make clear. "What I'm trying to say—"

Lacey didn't give him a chance to finish. "What you're saying is that romance is a frivolous pastime and women are shallow creatures easily taken in by how a man smells rather than how he treats others. Is he honest, moral, an ethical guy? Does he love or beat his dog? Is he so self-absorbed he doesn't see there are others less fortunate in his community?"

She glued him in place with a satisfied smirk. His pulse took a leap.

Whoa there, buddy boy. Zane couldn't buy it. "I don't see women as shallow at all. They're smart, funny, and tough. They live longer than men. What I can't figure out is why they leave their future happiness to the vulgarities of an archaic idea that has been taken over by a well-paid marketing industry."

Lacey's topaz eyes narrowed and not in a good way.

Valerie's Cheshire-cat grin grew wider, also a bad

sign.

Zane gave clearing the air another shot. "All I'm saying is propagating the species is a very biological function. Finding someone who could be a compatible mate would be so much easier if men and women understood the process."

"So opening doors, sending flowers and hand written notes, taking walks on the beach, going out to dinner, dancing—that's all a waste of time because it doesn't matter?"

Lacey's calm question had him understanding what it felt like to stand in the eye of a tornado, but she appeared to get his explanation. That was good enough for him.

"So, what you're saying is, all the girl has to do is find the one guy whose smell doesn't repulse her and she's set for life. She's found the man of her dreams, has she?"

Okay. Maybe he was wrong. That wasn't sugar and spice and all things nice she was tossing all over his valuable research.

His blood pulsed in sync with the sound of her voice. If his livelihood wasn't on the line, he might not ignore the sudden impulse to catch the golden-brown curl escaping the haphazard knot of her hair to fall near the crook of her slender neck.

"Exactly," he agreed instead, crossing his fingers he wasn't about to get into another pointless discussion with the woman who smelled like apple blossoms and vanilla. Could he replicate that scent, perhaps add a hint of illusive lavender that reminded him of his opponent?

She didn't give him time to bask in useless hope or do much more than wonder if he could create a scent that was uniquely Lacey Daniels. Though her lips smiled—lips he had a hard time looking away from—a tiny frown formed between perfect brows. "That is the biggest load of bunk I've ever heard."

"It's not bunk—"

"Now Lacey, Zane," Valerie interrupted what looked like it could turn into a squabble in front all of Portland and maybe more, a misstep that wouldn't help his short or long term plans. It wasn't until the morning show host turned to the audience with a smug smile that Zane knew he hadn't escaped disaster. "Our esteemed guests have different approaches to finding the perfect mate. How do we find out which one is right?"

"I can prove it." Zane spoke too quickly, a mistake he realized as his stomach sank at the triumph turning up the corners of Valerie's mouth.

"He can prove it, folks. What do you think? Shall we give the man a chance to show us science knows more than the human heart?"

"No!" He and Lacey, who'd scooted to the edge of her seat, objected at the same time.

The audience overruled them both, thundering its approval in applause loud enough to make Zane wince.

Valerie ran with the idea like an out-of-control horse heading for the barn. "How about a competition? Science versus romance? Raise your hands if you'd like to see a contest between our two guests."

The audience hooted and stomped their feet, some raising both hands.

Valerie looked like she was about to have an orgasm right there. "Lacey has to agree to participate. If she doesn't, we'll assume underneath her quest for romance she agrees with Zane; that she and her comic friends are frauds."

Beside him Lacey flinched, then lifted her delicate chin. He might disagree with her, but she was no fraud.

"So what do you think friends? Shall we give Zane two weeks to prove his theory that women choose their man based on his smell?" A ground-swell of approval rolled off the audience. Valerie talked right over them. "The rules are simple. Zane can try anything he creates in his lab to help him find a guy Lacey would consider spending the rest of her life with, but he can't use romance or any romantic gestures. No flowers. No chocolates. No cozy walks along the river. A scent he creates just for our girl here."

What the heck? Those rules hadn't come out of thin air. Valerie was too quick to rattle them off. And the challenge was darn close to the article he'd read that morning, Ted Connors' latest swipe at his book in the *Portland Times*.

Valerie shot Lacey a got-ya look. "If he succeeds our romance queen will make a public apology in her comic."

Lacey pressed kissable lips together—no, no, of course he didn't want to kiss his opponent—and began shaking her head, but then her apparent refusal to play Valerie's crazy game turned into reluctant nodding.

Don't do it. Stay strong. He sent the mental message realizing the same could be said to the scientist in the equation. Backed into a corner, he blurted out, "Wait. Two weeks isn't long enough."

Lacey folded her hands in her lap. Dark brows shot up as she gave him a look he recognized from his married friends.

What are you doing? The silent communication sprouting between them startled Zane and felt somehow…right…in an awkward kind of way. And it had to stop before he had one more girl in his life to worry about. Marriage had no place in his future.

Valerie held up a hand to quiet the enthusiastic audience. "I think two weeks is the perfect amount of time for our friends here to prove their points, don't you, folks?"

The audience jumped on the roller-coaster ride with Valerie, and Zane found a new loathing for being cornered into participating in the show host's insane contest, but what else could he do? What was Lacey going to do?

"If Zane doesn't succeed in winning Lacey over to his way of thinking, he'll take out a full page ad in the newspaper of Lacey's choice admitting romance trumps science any day of the week. We'll have a party to share the results right here on *Rise and Shine City Of Roses.*"

Lacey cast him a reckless look that didn't bode well for the two of them taking a united stand against Valerie's manipulation. If that was the way she wanted it, he'd be happy to oblige, because the truth was he had to win this stupid challenge. He needed solid book sales for his plans to click into place. When that happened taking care of Beth and Hannah would be a walk in the park.

Taking the bull by the horns, he arched his brows and jumped into the deep end. "I can prove my hypothesis, so I'm willing to take on this challenge...if you are."

Valerie and her audience faded into the background as Lacey met his gaze and flashed a smile of warning. "In two weeks? You're right. Can't be done. It takes that long just to get past the introductions."

"Afraid?" he suggested in a low, taunting tone.

"Not for a minute." Her sudden laugh put more than

his competitive nature on alert. How was it that he liked the idea of the lady making him work hard for his victory?

"You heard it here first, folks. The contest is on. Romance versus science. Who's going to be the winner, the girl or the boy?" Valerie raised her glass of water in a toast. "Let the mating game begin. And for our home audience, be sure to tune in next week as we follow Zane and Lacey's progress."

SIX

"WE'RE ALMOST THERE!" HANNAH SANG. The girl's excitement over their visit to the Portland Art Museum would have been contagious if Lacey wasn't still reeling from being pushed into participating in Valerie Simon's *mating game*.

She stared at the passing city blocks but didn't see the different neighborhoods the commuter train passed through, only her faint reflection looking back at her from the window. She'd wanted to become a household name, but not because she'd been cornered into a stupid, unworkable contest. And then this morning when she'd stumbled from bed, she'd found an email from Fran. Romance versus science had gone viral on the internet.

Getting into a debate with Zane on live television hadn't been her original plan or her finest hour, but here she was having to deal with the fallout. She chewed her lower lip. Fran, of course and why not, was pleased as punch *Love Lessons 101* was taking off.

Why didn't she share her boss' bounding enthusiasm? Probably because it wasn't Fran who had to go on date after date with strangers while the Professor attempted to seduce her with a manufactured scent created so she could smell her way to happiness.

Unfortunately, it wasn't totally Zane's fault she'd gotten caught up in Valerie's shenanigans. From the moment she'd given into his glib, *afraid?*—it was all on her.

Still, she liked the idea of readers talking up the comic; would even go out with Zane to prove she was right about couples and romance, if that's what it took to get Ge and the gang in the national spotlight.

To have Zane create a special scent for her so she could find a man, while insulting, did kind of make her tingle. What woman wouldn't love to have a man's undivided attention, except this man wanted to give her away, not keep her. Not that she was his to give away in the first place, or that she wanted him to keep her...whatever that meant.

Ugh! It was all very confusing and made her more determined than ever to prove she was right about couples and romance. If she could convince Valerie's audience and anyone else paying attention that the Professor was wrong about his so called theory, she would win Valerie's contest. There was only one stumbling block she was having trouble getting past. A startling attraction for Beth's brother it seemed she couldn't rationalize or dismiss.

"Our stop's next." Hannah hopped across the aisle and plopped down next to Lacey on the sideways facing bench. "We saw you and Uncle Zane on television yesterday."

Lacey laughed and with an eye-rolling look in Beth's direction said tongue-in-cheek, "Yeah, that was awesome, wasn't it?"

Beth leaned into the conversation. "For a moment there I thought you and Zane were going to tell Valerie Simons to shove—" She glanced at her daughter who was hanging on every word. "—That you weren't going to play her game."

Lacey knew the exact moment Beth was referring to and would have sworn she and Zane were on the same page, too. Something silent...and yummy...*had* passed between them. But then he'd asked if she was afraid. To stand up for her principles? Was the guy nuts? Of course she wasn't afraid.

"I thought about it. Not sure about your brother."

Since he'd left without saying a word, she had to assume he was already working on a plan to find her mythical guy. His intentional jab at the end of the show made her reckless, and restless, keeping her awake last night brainstorming three new ideas for Georgette and the Professor's next few escapades.

Did the fun she had playing Ge against the Professor's improbable dating methods make her a bad person or was she having fun because she actually liked Zane Tyler, and not just in a I-want-to-be-your-friend-way?

"We're here!" Hannah grabbed her hand and jumped up, dragging Lacey off the train. "Come on. I don't want to miss anything."

"Hannah, slow down," Beth said on a laugh.

A long banner announced the newest show that had Hannah so excited. It was an exhibit by the renowned animation studio, LAIKA. The girl wanted to be a photographer. Lacey understood. That's how she was about being a cartoon artist. Even before her differing opinion with Zane had blown up into a thing, Georgette and Frank, and now the Professor, could completely take over every minute of her day.

She frowned. Ever since her breakup with Stephen, she'd dedicated every minute she could to Ge and the gang. That was a good thing. Wasn't it?

Linking arms, Beth sandwiched Hannah between them as they headed toward the grand entrance of the museum. A sudden pang of envy nailed Lacey. Someday she'd love to have a daughter like Beth's with whom she could share everything, including the success of *Love Lessons*.

Finding a man who wanted a child too wouldn't be easy. Who did she even know? An image of Zane popped into her mind. He wasn't the one, with his crazy mating ideas, but maybe going on dates as he attempted to prove his point wasn't a horrible idea. It was one way to get back in the dating game.

She could practice her romance on the very handsome Zane and after winning his apology, go on a few dates of her own choosing; perhaps even find a guy who was interested in a lifetime commitment and eventually a family.

"Uncle Zane!" Hannah rushed into her uncle's waiting arms.

Lacey stayed back, heart skipping a few beats as the man inhabiting too much of her thought time lifted his niece in a huge hug and swung her in a circle that left the girl's legs dangling. A smacking kiss was deposited on Hannah's temple as she squealed in delight.

"You didn't tell me this was a family outing." The moisture gathering in her eyes had nothing to do with Zane Tyler, the scientist, and everything to do with the uncle who was taking time away from his lab to spend the day with his niece in a stuffy museum. "I should go."

Beth grabbed her hand. "Stay. It was Zane's idea to invite you. Not that we wouldn't have anyway."

Lacey shot her friend a skeptical scowl.

"I guess I forgot to mention that, didn't I?" Beth

shrugged. "Actually, he asked me not to tell you until we got here."

Zane put his niece down. "Hi, Lacey."

All her good feelings for the man evaporated. "So you arranged this little social gathering?"

"Yes, Hannah was sure she could talk you into coming." A wink of conspiracy passed between uncle and niece. What was the world coming to when you couldn't trust a sweet ten year-old? "How about we all go to dinner after we check out the museum? My treat."

Why was she upset an unexpected excursion to the museum with her friends had turned out to be something else. It wasn't like Zane was *the one*. She knew he wanted to *talk*. And after what happened on *Rise and Shine City of Roses* they *had* to talk.

"I can't."

"Of course you can. You cleared your calendar, remember?" the traitor Beth said, tugging her into the red-brick building housing the museum's treasures.

Lacey resisted, but then gave in. Isn't this what she wanted? An opportunity to try out her romancing moves—okay not those kind of moves—on the man following them into the museum?

Several hours later, after wandering through displays of animated art and technology, unable to take her eyes off Zane and how he genuinely liked spending time with Beth and Hannah, she sighed like a lovesick heroine in one of her favorite romance novels. Amazed—it was just so sexy—at how he dealt with his girls, she couldn't help wondering how special it would be to become part of that exclusive circle. Would he use all his power for good to make love last forever? Or after getting what he wanted would he disappear and never look back?

Do you want to be one of his girls?

Fighting a thrill, she stopped to stare at a detailed ink drawing not part of the LAIKA exhibit. A woman peered from behind robed men, the intimate mix of black, rose, and leaf-green watery inks blending in perfect, peaceful harmony.

Dang it, she wanted that harmony. And she wanted that harmonious moment for a lifetime with—

"I'm not sorry we got you here under false pretenses. You've been a hard woman to pin down."

—instead of hiding in her apartment and letting Georgette and Frank be her face to the world.

She turned to face Zane. He'd snuck up on her in more ways than catching her admiring an enlightening piece of exquisite art. "You had this planned before yesterday's show, didn't you?"

"I thought it would be a good opportunity to explain. But we missed that boat, didn't we?" His crooked grin tugged at the confused girl inside. Not good.

The way Zane's lips twitched reminded her of the sheepish look her dad gave her mom when he was doing his best to get back in his wife's good graces. Butterflies fluttered in Lacey's belly.

He leaned close and breathed in. Distraction deepened his voice. "Apple? Spice?"

Startled at the desire reeling her in the wrong direction, she couldn't deny the man was so likable. Her eyes crossed, but she got out words that sounded close to normal. She hoped. "Apple blossom body lotion. I made it myself."

"Really?" Zane's gaze refocused on her face, losing none of its intensity.

"It's a hobby." She managed to edge toward the

museum's reception area. Now was not the time to get waylaid by the spark of sudden interest in a hunky guy's eyes gone soft. "People have hobbies, you know."

"Of course they do. I just thought yours was that comic you write."

That was all it took. Despite how smart he was, the man didn't have a brain in his head. And for a minute there she'd thought—damn, what had she been thinking? "Okay. On that happy little judgment, I'm out of here."

"Wait. I didn't mean—"

"Uncle Zane, I'm hungry."

Thank you, Hannah. Saved by the voracious appetite of a ten-year-old.

"You're always hungry." Zane wrapped his niece in a snug hug, but his gaze remained on Lacey's face. "Come with us. There's a great pizza place close by."

She shook her head. "I can't. Too much work to do on that little hobby of mine."

He winced and then half laughed. "Don't deprive yourself of a free lunch just because I managed to be an ass. Again."

"Uncle Zane!" Hannah scolded.

He scrubbed the top of his niece's head with his knuckles. "Sorry, kiddo. Next time I'll say donkey's behind."

Hannah grinned and nodded. "That's better."

God, he was adorable. *Get out while you still can, woman.*

As much as she liked him, there was no going back to the point when they were just a boy and a girl bumping into each other in a college parking lot. She had to see Valerie's contest through. There was too much riding on the outcome—her future, career, and the future of her so-called hobby.

She gestured in the direction of the exit. "I've got to get going."

"Tomorrow then. Dinner?" Zane grabbed her hand and at the tingling warmth igniting where their palms came together she almost gave in to his invitation. When he let her hand go, she could breathe again. "I need time to work on the scent that will be the most attractive to you, I can't get started until I figure out what tastes and smells excite you."

Keeping Valerie's mating game front and center was probably smart, though his dedication to victory stung a little. It would be better for her piece of mind if *she* picked the time and place. The sooner they got this ridiculous...thing...over with, the sooner they could both go back to their normal lives.

Lacey crossed her arms over her chest. "Shall we consider this our first date?"

"No."

Okay then. "Lunch. Twelve o'clock. Papa Haydn in Sellwood."

Zane waited at the window table he'd been shown to, drumming his fingers on the white table cloth. The restaurant was famous for its desserts, but they served meals too.

His chest tightened. The woman was clever picking Papa Haydn with its romantic table settings and decadent desserts. In fact, too clever for his piece of mind. After picking up a copy of that morning's *Oregon Tribune*—his jaw ached from grinding his molars after reading the latest installment of her comic—he was flat out determined to discover something that would put her in a cooperative mood.

In her depiction of their encounter on the *Rise and Shine City of Roses* stage, underneath her snarky humor Lacey was almost as harsh as Ted Connors. Except, he smiled as he admitted he found the woman intriguing even when she was holding him over a barrel in front of hundreds, maybe even millions of readers who likely wouldn't buy his book now.

He opened the newspaper he'd brought to the comic section and read again the recap of the morning show debacle. Georgette and the Professor were funny, though he didn't remember Lacey fluttering long eyelashes at him to get his attention. If he remembered right, and he did, she'd glared disbelieving at him every time he tried to explain his theory. The lady was a tough customer. Why had she agreed to participate in Valerie's mating game?

He glanced at his watch. She wasn't late. Yet.

Continuing to study her drawings, he tried to understand Lacey's motivation. Surely she didn't need to win this contest more than he did. If she did win, it would be disastrous.

It wasn't that he didn't trust her to follow through with Valerie's rules of engagement—Beth had lots of good things to say about her neighbor—but other than his sister's word, what did he really know about Lacey except what he could see with his own eyes.

She was smart, beautiful, a very talented cartoonist. And she was a throwback to a time when people believed in the mythology of the heart over the logic of the head. He had to convince the lady his theory on how to pick the right guy was right.

He glanced at his watch again. Now she was late.

Had she decided to stand him up?

"More coffee, sir?"

"Yes, thanks."

The bright-eyed innocence of the twenty-some-thing girl who was his waitress had him wishing, just this once, that Lacey was equally uncomplicated. The least she could do was have the decency to keep their appointment...date...whatever.

Abby, according to her name tag, refilled his cup. "Do you want to order?"

"I'll wait a little longer."

Abby retreated behind the counter displaying the dessert choices just as Lacey walked through the door. She quickly scanned the room.

Zane rose, lifting a hand so she would see him, then watched as with a graceful stride she cut through the tables scrunched close in the small dining room. Her hair was tangled in a knot at the back of her neck, a favored style he noticed and couldn't help wondering what it would be like to unwind the bun. A long-sleeved, red sweater hung to mid-thigh, black legging showing off long, perfect legs. He shook his head in regret. Now was not the time to yield to the lady's mystery.

Hoping a show of manners would impress his lunch companion and make her more amenable to the plan he'd formulated, he pulled out her chair, tucking her close to the table once she'd sat down.

"Sorry I'm late. I had a stop to make before I came." She cast him an apologetic look, reminding him all over again that despite their differences, she was a fascinating woman.

"No problem." He signaled the waitress.

She surprised him by offering a red rose tied with a

white ribbon. Confused, Zane frowned. Roses, red or any other color, were not on his agenda. "What's this?"

"A rose." Her laugh was infectious, igniting an insane curiosity he couldn't afford.

He placed the stunning flower on the table between them. His pulse picked up a beat. No one had given him flowers before. "I know it's a rose. My question is why?"

"Just because." The quick quirk of her lips trampled on his determination to keep to the business reasons for their lunch.

Abby came to take their order. When she left, he lifted the nearest corner of the paper under his elbow and served up his first observation to see what excuse the cagey woman would counter with. "This isn't very flattering."

She shrugged. "Ge doesn't like the Professor much."

"Why is she flirting with him if she doesn't like him?"

Lacey stirred cream into her coffee. "She wants to see what he has up his sleeve."

"Is that why you brought me a rose? To see what I have up my sleeve?"

It wasn't hard to see her fictional characters were a reflection of him and Lacey and their current conflict. She was ingenious, actually. And sitting across the table from her, occupied in normal conversation—or as close to normal as they'd gotten so far—made it harder to stay focused.

Their food arrived. Lacey spread the napkin in her lap. "So what's next?"

Direct and to the point, he liked that in a woman. Especially his women. Scratch that. Lacey was not his woman. "I start working on your scent first thing in the morning."

Her brow wrinkled delightfully, giving him a kick in the gut. "Not perfume for me to wear."

"No, a cologne for men."

"Right, because it's the *man's* smell that will cause me to throw all my good sense out the window and fall in love with some guy who doesn't have the same interests I do, or who doesn't want the same things I want. Quick, where do we find these fabulous science experiments?"

If he was looking for a love interest, which he wasn't, not until Beth and Hannah were well taken care of anyway, Lacey, with her quirky sense of humor and opinionated censure would be at the top of a very short list. She was one of a kind, and he was in a lot of trouble.

"Cute. Under the terms of our agreement—" Feminine brows arched. "All right…Valerie's challenge—"

"*Mating game.*"

"Fine. Mating game." Zane couldn't get the words out with Lacey's suddenly curious gaze settled on his face. "The guy who knocks your socks off is to be wearing the scent I make."

"I get that part. What I want to know is how you plan to pull off this charade?" She leaned on her elbow, chin in hand, intent gaze flashing amusement.

Zane cleared his throat. She'd ordered the Baked Mac 'n' Cheese. She liked comfort food. Good to know. "My first thought was to have you go to a singles bar."

"No."

He held up a hand to stop further protest. Lacey wrinkled her nose, another good thing to know. She didn't like blatant trolling.

"Now I'm thinking maybe a pub or dance club

would be better. Do you dance?"

She gave him a thoughtful, not so innocent look. "If you call having a spaz attack dancing."

She was kidding, he hoped, and wasn't going to like this next part. "My plan was to pick three guys to wear the cologne I create—"

She put her fork down. "They'd all smell the same. I don't see how that will prove your theory."

"Good point, except as long as the product isn't put on with a heavy hand, body chemistry has a huge effect on fragrance. There should be subtle differences in how the guys smell that you'll either respond to or not."

"You're making that up." Lacey pushed her plate away before leaning on her crossed arms, giving him a sexy view. On purpose or not, it made him dizzy.

"No, it's true," Zane jerked his gaze up to her face and choked out a credible laugh. He hoped. "Cross my heart, but it doesn't matter. I've changed my mind. I'm starting to think you're more complex than standing at the head of a receiving line and shaking hands with a long line of men who are strangers."

Eyebrows arching and the corners of her lips quirking in amusement, Lacey leaned closer. "Thank you. I think."

Keeping his gaze elevated, he took a reviving breath and continued, "I've decided to go with one guy, hide him in the crowd, then encourage several to stop by your table."

"Isn't that like stacking the deck? What if I don't like your guy?"

"Not stacked at all. You won't know who he is and you don't have to take him home, just decide to go on a second date." Zane was surprised by the sudden knot in his gut. The idea of Lacey going on dates with another man, let alone taking him home, stole his appetite.

Brushing aside the inconvenient pit in his stomach, he was glad he already had the perfect guy in mind. Brian owed him a favor. And his best friend wasn't looking for any long term entanglements, which was fortunate. It wasn't the guy who had to make the moves, it was Lacey.

Brian was a safe bet.

"I've made a list of rules." From beneath the newspaper he pulled out a sheet of paper.

Lacey picked up her fork, the tines pointed in his direction. "Rules?"

"That's right." He pointed at the flower on the table, unaccountably pleased she'd thought to flatter him with a gift. "No roses. No romantic gimmicks at all. No sabotage. Just come to the club. Let the guys approach without scaring them off. Dance a little. Have fun. Stay open to finding the *one*. It'll all be over before you know it."

"Huh. You think so?" She scooped cheesy pasta into her mouth.

"Absolutely." Zanc couldn't take his eyes off the slow slide of the fork coming from between her lips. "You'll have your man. I'll get a retraction and be back in my lab as if this little hiccup had never happened."

She nudged the rose toward him and had the audacity to wink. "We'll see about that."

SEVEN

LACEY STUDIED THE CROWD FILLING the tables and bar area and didn't see anything in the man department that rang her chimes except the tall drink of water leaning on the bar hocking her like she was some kind of hot tamale he was super-anxious to hand off to someone else.

With its intimate setting, Studio 13, a new dance and social club in Portland's Pearl District, seemed the perfect place for Zane to prove or disprove his position. The summer night air was warm, lighting romantically low, and the band mellow. Patrons spilled into the walled-in courtyard off the dance floor.

She sighed, dispirited. All she had to do was get through the evening with her dignity intact. And...not let her frustration over his *rules* spill over onto the guys sent to take her for a spin on the dance floor.

While getting dressed that night she'd decided there were some rules Zane apparently didn't know. Hence the short sapphire dress, gladiator sandals, hair loose and hanging down her back, makeup perfectly applied. She'd been rewarded for her extra efforts by the widening of his expressive eyes before recovering.

She twirled the short glass of Bailey's and cream between slender fingers. The Professor was just trying to prove a point. It was only fair to give him this chance since after her conversation with his sister, she'd pretty much decided it was pointless to give him another. She would never change his mind.

While Hannah was at her first sleep over with a friend last night, Beth had told her all about Nanette's pursuit of the perfect guy while ignoring her children. What his mother had done was all about self-indulgence, not romance, but Zane would never believe her version after what he'd witnessed as a kid.

And if, by some remote chance, there was some validity to his notion that fragrances mixing with body chemistry played a major roll in finding the right partner? Ridiculous, of course, but the idea had nonetheless nagged her ever since their lunch meeting.

He was right. The sooner they finished this experiment of his, the sooner they could both go about their normal lives. There was one small problem. She enjoyed Georgette's and the Professor's ongoing disagreement and needed to see that story-line through, which was one of the reasons she'd shown up tonight. That and the invitation to the reunion still sitting on her desk. Maybe she'd actually meet someone who could go as her date.

Impatient, she shifted. She'd intercepted a few interested looks, but no takers so far. Was she trying too hard to be interested in the band? Pushing her empty glass to the center of the table, she rested her chin in her hand. A shadow fell across the table. Ah ha, success at last.

When she looked up she fell deep into a familiar blue-gray gaze. Zane offered a second drink.

"I don't think a woman drinking herself into a stupor is quite the image you're going for."

That brought on one of his sexy frowns, which perked her up right away. Just to test his will power, she placed a hand on her abdomen just below the girls she flatteringly exposed by her best push-up bra.

She looked down to emphasize her point. "Is there something wrong with my dress or is this exercise just a science experiment gone wrong?"

Placing the drink on the table with a little more force than was necessary, she thought, he claimed her free hand and pulled her from the chair. "Dance with me."

The joke was on her. Before she could catch her breath, she was on the dance floor. Strong, muscular arms, for a science-guy, tugged her close, making her feel safe and protected, which she didn't need. She was an independent woman. Still, it felt good to be held close to the guy who had no clue he was waking up her engine.

The seductive tones of an alto sax lured her close to Zane as he wove her around the other dancers. If she hadn't been super-attracted before, she was now. The man definitely had dancing skills.

"What are we doing?"

"Giving you curb appeal." His breath brushed her cheek, the hand holding her close splayed wide on the small of her back.

Lacey tried to laugh off his odd choice of metaphors. All that came out was a strangled snort. "As in *beautiful house on the outside; don't know what's on the inside, but let's get into a bidding war?*"

The muscle along his jaw flexed. Zane nodded, a slow smile molding his tempting lips, "That's the general idea."

She opened her mouth to say something...anything...

but her words got tangled. Definitely not amused, she shook her head. "It won't work."

"We'll see." He dipped her over his arm. "Play nice."

If someone had told her a month ago she'd find a pushy, cheeky man fascinating, she would have categorically denied it. She didn't want another Stephen, though Zane was nothing like her ex.

He returned her to safe footing, thank goodness, and brushed a loose strand of hair behind her ear. As awareness took a romping road trip down her spine ending in a puddle in her girl parts, the moment stretched out. She blinked at the tug on her senses and held her breath. A hint of woods and sexy man almost made her forget why they were there in the first place.

Yup, she'd better stop ogling her competitor and give his hookup method her best effort. No way did she want to admit to Valerie Simons and all her viewers, much less Zane, that she was falling for the science-guy. If she had to do that, she might as well put *Love Lessons* on the back shelf and open a new startup company setting up arranged marriages.

A tap on her shoulder brought her back to earth. "Can I cut in?"

The question, drawled low, came from a blonde Greek god with amused green eyes and the build of a long distance runner. He was dressed in jeans and a black button down shirt, suitable armor for a social club.

Staring at Zane, Lacey decided she needed armor of her own. He might be right about the bidding war, but he didn't look happy that it appeared his strategy had worked. "Sure."

Surprising, he didn't let her go. Was his reluctance part of the game? Now who was breaking the rules?

She gave a small push and shot him a look that told Zane to get lost. "Thanks for the dance."

Ignoring his odd behavior she turned to the new guy. "I'm Lacey."

"Brian." He swung her into a fast two-step.

It didn't escape her attention that Zane hadn't gone far. She smiled at her partner like she'd been waiting for him all night. "So, what do you do, Brian?"

The dam broke. Time whirled by as she danced with a different guy almost every dance. Brian made way for Alex. Alex conceded to Ryan.

The whole time Zane hovered on the sidelines, at one point bringing her another drink. She handed the Bailey's back. "Two's enough for me, thanks," then mouthed, *go away.*

She stopped trying to get names and hoped Zane was happy with the results. So far not one of her partners tripped her trigger. The disconcerting part was all night she knew where her partner in crime loitered, even while dancing with strangers.

Partner in crime?

Feeling foolish, but so she could say she hadn't sabotaged his precious results, she subtly smelled each of her dance partners. If she happened to sneak in a question or two eliciting some telling information about her dance partner, just to make their conversation easier, she wasn't going to be the one to tell Zane.

At the end of more dances than she could count, she ended up at a table with three of the most promising gents lounging around competing for her attention like she was a football they wanted to carry across the goal line. Alex, Brian, and Hank, all nice guys, but not one grabbed her attention over the others.

She caught Zane's eye as he watched from the bar. In

that heartbeat she understood. She was tired, her feet hurt, it was time to go home.

Brian took her hand, pulling her to her feet. "Another dance?"

"You're sweet, but no. I'm done for the night."

"Can I make sure you get home okay?"

Maybe Brian was a player. Maybe he was a nice guy. The truth was she had no desire to find out. In a blinding realization, she knew why. He wasn't Zane, who at that moment was staring into the drink in front of him on the bar.

"That's okay. I have my car."

Brian pulled a business card from his pocket. Alex and Hank wandered off to find better amusement, not that she blamed them. "It was good to meet you, Lacey Daniels. I hope you'll call. I'd love to take you to dinner, or something."

It was the *or something* she wasn't interested in pursuing with this man.

Zane caught her at the door. "You're leaving? But—"

She took a fortifying breath. What else was a girl to do who'd just realized she'd fallen head over heels for the wrong man? She lifted her chin and told a lie.

"I'm exhausted." That much was the truth. Careful not to give away her stunning revelation, she stood still while Zane studied her face before adding what had to be said. "There's no one here I want to take home or ask on a date."

"No one?"

"No one."

"Let's meet tomorrow at Daily in the Pearl. We'll make plans to try again."

"Why?" Lacey closed her eyes and blew out a breath. She couldn't spend another night wanting one man while he wanted her to pick another. And she wasn't about to discuss all that in a social club, which should have been the perfect place to *find a mate*, but wasn't. "Fine. What time?"

"Eleven?" Zane's expression edged into concern. "Are you okay?"

"Just tired."

"See you tomorrow?"

Never expecting to fall for the Professor and rattled because she was standing on shaky ground, she nodded.

The drive home was short, which was good since she didn't want to think about...anything. Without turning on the lights she stumbled into her bedroom and stripped down to her underclothes. It was too hot for a blanket so she crawled into bed and curled into a ball.

Attraction was one thing. Giving away her heart was another. Lacey pulled the sheet over her head.

She had *not* fallen in love with Mr. Zane *choose-your-mate-by-his-smell* Tyler.

An amused, nagging voice in her head, Georgette's no doubt, whispered...*wanna bet*?

EIGHT

WAITING FOR LACEY AT THE Daily, Zane scrubbed eyes dry from lack of sleep. Studio 13 had been a bust, in more ways than one. Lacey was mad. The woman didn't know how to be subtle about her feelings. It was as clear as day by the set of her shoulders when she'd unceremoniously dumped him at the club.

The good news was the call he'd gotten that morning from his editor. Since the show had aired, sales for his book had soared. It turned out folks liked watching a train wreck and would happily pay for the privilege. The bad news? He'd wanted Lacey to like his cologne on Brian and therefore prove his theory. For reasons he couldn't explain he no longer cared if the cologne worked or not.

Frowning, he ordered black coffee and a vanilla latte with whipped cream—comfort food she would appreciate—then picked a table in the farthest corner, out of the way of folks waiting in line to place their orders. He put the latte and a small box of chocolates he'd picked up in front of the empty chair on the other side of the small table. Settling in to wait, he wasn't sure what message he was trying to send with the salted caramels, but hoped Lacey would appreciate his gesture to smooth things over.

Everything had been going according to plan last night until, unable to stay away from the mesmerizing sound of her voice, he'd taken her that last drink. She was focused on Brian and the other two guys flirting with her. She'd danced several dances with his friend which appeared to put Brian in the favorite slot ahead of the others. It was what he thought he wanted.

It wasn't; not if the sick feeling in his gut was anything to go by. When he'd backed off, stunned by the jealousy crippling his logic and the reasons why he'd gone along with Valerie's *game*, she'd called it quits.

Zane shook his head at the confused stupidity that had him giving her the bums' rush to get a commitment to meet for a regroup. By the time he'd finished babbling, she wasn't happy and he wasn't sure she would actually come to the coffee shop.

An instinct that was becoming attuned to Lacey's presence had him looking toward the entrance. The look on the pretty face of the lady winding her way through the tables said she was still angry. Scrounging up a careless smile, he jumped to his feet, pulled out her chair, and with the non-skills of a randy teenager, blurted, "You're beautiful."

The words shocked him as much as they did her, but he wouldn't take them back. She *was* beautiful and not just because he needed her willing participation to finish their contest.

Expression blanking, she sank into the chair and picked up the gold wrapped box. "What's this? I thought you said no romance. First a compliment, then—" She turned the box over, then over again so the red bow was on top. "Chocolates?"

"Not romance, I swear. An apology of sorts. I didn't

intend for you to actually take a guy home last night."

"I know." Her lips flattened as she studied the box of candy a moment longer before setting it back on the table unopened.

He reached for her hand. "But you're mad. Why?"

Wary caution replaced the anger. She dodged his question. "Which one of those guys was your dark horse?"

He hadn't factored in that the night would end without his desired results, at the very least Lacey leaving the club with a new boyfriend. And he hadn't anticipated it would turn out *he,* appearing to have lost his marbles, wanted to be that boyfriend.

Since he'd seen Brian slip Lacey his business card, hand lingering far longer than was necessary on hers, maybe it would be better not to make her anger worse by revealing the truth of how he felt about last night's outcome. "Brian is a friend of mine."

"I see. So the honorable Professor used a friend and gave him the inside track."

The accusation made him uncomfortable and left him without a valid excuse except for his loyalty to Beth and Hannah. The only defense he could come up with was he'd agreed to Valerie's plan when Lacey was a stranger and before he'd gotten to know her as a woman, who underneath all the romantic bluster, was smart, sassy, and worth seeing if there was more to uncover.

"Brian's one of the good guys. I didn't think it could hurt to see if my cologne would make him more attractive—"

"—To me." Lacey drank her coffee but her unwavering stare was a sure sign he wasn't earning any points.

And he wasn't going to if he couldn't understand her

side of the equation. His first attempt at executing the scent he'd created for her failed. Maybe not the scent, but the execution? Was it because she wasn't the kind of girl who went looking for a lifelong partner, or even someone she could occasionally date, at a social club.

The real reason Brian had been such a good idea was because his buddy was a safe bet. If he'd chosen a stranger to wear the cologne anything could have happened, none of it good.

Zane's palms broke out in a sweat as he realized Lacey was as important to him as Beth and Hannah, and even more important than his work. When had they, at least on his part, gone from rivals to something more...chummy?

"How close is your lab?"

Still caught up in the revelation he had crossed the line from competitor to wanting a more personal relationship with Lacey, Zane muttered, "A few blocks away."

Grabbing her coffee and box of chocolates, she stood. "I'd like to see it, if you don't mind."

She wasn't kidding. He couldn't think of a good reason not to show her where he worked and lived when he wasn't looking after his sister and niece, or making deals to secure their future, or participating in Valerie's crazy *mating* game, or falling in love—

"I don't mind." Zane's breath lodged in his chest. He couldn't possibly be falling for the woman waiting for him to lead the way out of the coffee house. Infatuation had not snuck up without him knowing. Besides, showing Lacey his lab was just another opportunity to see what scents moved the lady.

She was quiet on the short walk. Three blocks later he let them into the renovated warehouse that was part lab and part living area. The expansive room he hadn't sectioned off into smaller rooms had high open ceilings and exposed duct work. Light filtered in from a bank of divided windows along the wall that faced the street. Work stations were scattered across the open room.

Lacey drew in a quick breath. "Nice space."

He agreed. "It works."

"I can see why."

She left her coffee and box of chocolates on the first workstation, wandering from one station to the next. Itching to flaunt the place he loved, Zane couldn't take his gaze away from the woman taking a tour of his personal domain.

She ended up back where she started—at the workstation where he waited. "Beth says you live upstairs?"

"That's right. I wanted to be close to work and the extra space in the warehouse made that possible."

"Show me."

What guy wouldn't want Lacey Daniels checking out his home, but was it just plain curiosity or something else that had her asking to see his private space? "Okay, but why?"

"You want to know what made me mad last night?"

Curiosity, and maybe a good dose of lust for the woman getting the better of him, Zane led the way to the elevator that would take them upstairs. Once there, like the lab, the space was open, windows large, the walls made from the red brick of the brewery that was the building's first incarnation.

He stopped in the main living area and faced Lacey. Time to find out if she had any idea why his cologne had failed. "So what do you think went wrong last night? And why were you mad at me, besides the fact that Georgette's trying to teach the Professor about romance and is not having much luck?"

His attempt at humor fell flat.

Placing her hands on each side of his face, she tugged him close until their breaths mingled, sending a silent shout of hoorah coursing through his blood stream. "I like you. And though I know you think you're trying to prove a point, I didn't like being traded on the open market like I was some prized possession. And just so we're clear, I don't like you because of the way you smell. I like you because of how you take care of Beth and Hannah, and because you buy a girl chocolates, and worry she might have gotten the wrong message."

Mixing business and pleasure was not good, but stunned at her admission, Zane closed the remaining distance, joining them in a kiss that made a five-point earthquake seem mild. Greedy fingers furrowed into his hair. Restraint hung on by a thread.

He didn't just like-like Lacey. He loved-liked her. "Wait."

She pulled back, eyes dark with passion glued to his face.

Lacey was a woman who deserved the whole parade and to know ahead of time what she was getting into. "I won't lie to you. I'm not in a position to promise forever or—"

A slender finger covered his mouth. "Shhhh."

That's all it took to crumble his good intentions. Picking up the stunning woman and without breaking the kiss that demanded all his passion, he carried her to the bedroom.

The anger that had kept her company all the way to

The Daily fizzled. She just couldn't keep it going in the face of Zane's worry because he couldn't figure out why she was mad. Regardless, he couldn't storm into her life, make havoc with his ill hatched theories, sexy walk, and the hint of musky earth and showered man that made her want to bury her nose against his skin. Who did he think he was? He couldn't just manipulate her for his own interests.

And she would tell him all that as soon as her fingers were done exploring the line of his jaw where his neck became strong shoulders and then tangled in the buttons of his shirt, a frustrating barrier to what lay hidden beneath. She pulled the offending shirt free of his pants so she could explore more, while clever hands drove her wild, paying her back in kind for her flagrant trespassing.

Zane Tyler took her breath away. So why in the heck was she fighting with the man? Because they had opposite opinions on how to go about finding the perfect life partner?

She wasn't fighting at the moment. Unless she counted this race to see who could get out of their clothes the quickest, a contest she was very inspired to win.

Her tunic came off. Zane skimmed her hips on the way to palming lace covered breasts. When he slipped off her bra, she vaguely wondered why she even cared that he believed the science of dating was more important than the romance itself.

Determined to be fair, she pulled back. "Is there a girlfriend who would object to me being here?"

"No girlfriend."

Pounding desire overrode every thought at his admission. "Good."

Clothes gone, her palms encountered chest hair and followed where it led to aroused, hard male. Splintered by texture and the need to touch every stunning inch of the man, the back of her knees met the bed. They tumbled and rolled until she was on top, evidence of his intentions pressing into her belly.

A slow and gentle introduction was all of a sudden the last thing she wanted. Lacey gasped, "Condom?"

Stretching, Zane pulled one from the side table drawer, giving her a perfect view of his impressive length. A breathless flutter joined the ache in her lady parts. Tearing the outer wrap, she rolled on the protection. Hard chest crushing her breasts, lean hips pushing into her, and mouth blazing a fiery trail, she tripped over the edge into a free fall Lacey wasn't sure she'd survive.

But survive she did. When she realized she hadn't perished from the heat burning like a firestorm between them, she was draped over his heaving chest, breathless, the texture of his chest hair tickling out the last of her climax. Strong arms bound her there. Hands skimming her back promised more. And, dang it, he smelled just fine.

Tugging the sheet to cover them both, voice rough with unspent passion, he said, "Tell me what you like."

I'm not in a position to promise forever.

"I, uh—" Pretty sure he wouldn't want to hear what she liked, what she'd just that moment realized she wanted more than anything, she kissed him. Hard.

This time their coming together was slow and thorough, a languorous exploration of the length and breadth of each other, as though they had all the time in the world. In her pounding heart Lacey knew better.

He stole her breath with the intensity of the attention he gave to discovering every part of her pulsing body and what made her hum; the way he took his time testing what pushed her pulse into overdrive, her back to arch and other parts to shudder.

Butterflies took flight, each carrying a small measure of how much she wanted this man in a way she'd never wanted Stephen. Hungry lips and busy hands carried her along until he took her unresisting, surfing a dangerous but thrilling wave that in the end had them crashing together.

Zane collapsed on her as she sought to catch her breath. Hoping it didn't sound like she was begging, she scraped words past her dry throat. "Can we do that again?"

"Uh huh."

But instead they dozed until she was awakened by gentle fingers stroking her temple and Zane's grumbled, "I have to go to work."

It took a minute for his words to sink in and then to understand what they meant.

Scrambling out of the bed, taking the sheet with her to cover the essentials gone cold, splashed with a sudden dose of freezing reality, her heart cracked. "Back to work on the scent that's supposed to make me attracted to another man? Is that the work you're talking about?"

His brows slammed together. "I—" More words didn't come.

Grabbing her clothes from the floor, Lacey headed for the nearest door which turned out to be a walk in closet.

"Lacey. Wait."

He hadn't lied. He'd warned her not to count on forever. It was her own fault she'd ignored the warning, thinking the few hours they'd spent entangled in his sheets meant something. Something important.

"Why?" She half-closed the closet door so he couldn't see how his quick return to where they were last night cut deep to the bone. He was wrong about romance and love, but she couldn't get the words past the lump in her throat.

The sound of footsteps on the hardwood floor approach the closet. "Can we talk?"

"There's nothing to talk about." Tugging her tunic down around her hips, the whisper of the fabric reminded her how intimate it felt to have Zane's hands there instead. She pushed the door open. "I am such a fool."

"You're not. It's me. I'm the fool." He'd found his clothes, at least his pants anyway.

He reached for her, but she sidestepped and made it to the other side of the bed while holding back the tears threatening to fall. "For Pete's sake, Zane. You're a smart man, but you're a moron. You have to know there are more important things a woman has to consider than how a guy smells."

She couldn't decide if she wanted to bop the Professor upside the head or run her hands through his chest hair one more time.

His handsome face took on a determined look as he came after her. Lacey retreated into the living area and into the elevator. He stopped a foot away when she hit the first floor button.

She waved a hand between them. "I'm done with this…this science experiment."

The elevator doors closed. And that was that.

The tears she'd been holding back by sheer will spilled over. Heart crumbling, Lacey let them fall.

NINE

ZANE SAT ON THE BED, elbows propped on his knees, head bowed and clutched in his hands. Lacey had left an hour ago and still he couldn't move. What had he done? Not the sex—that was...wow! There were no words to describe the pyrotechnics he and Lacey had set off together. No, that wasn't the problem.

The problem, beside the hard knot in his gut? He'd let her leave. Let the love of his life walk out of his home—and life, he was sure of it—without even trying to talk her into staying. And not for Valerie Simons' stupid, stupid contest, either. For them. For him.

As the elevator doors closed on the woman who'd managed against all of his rules to find space in his heart—he was flummoxed by the discovery—it became clear as the freckles on his niece's face that for the first time in his life, he was crazy in love. With Lacey Daniels. *And he didn't want to let her go.*

The ring of his cell broke through the remorse filling his chest. For a brief second he thought it was Lacey. Another woman's voice spoke in his ear. Lacey was right. He was a moron.

"Zane. How are you? This is Valerie Simons calling live from the studio of *Rise and Shine City of Roses.*"

Zane didn't want to play the show host's game anymore. Lacey was right. Where had it gotten them except—?

In your bed.

He abandoned the polite route. "Hello Valerie. What can I do for you?"

"So we're taping an afternoon show and the audience and I were having, you know, a little chat. We were wondering how things are going between you and Lacey. So I said why don't we just pick up the phone and ask? Any news would be good news," the woman purred.

Grinding his molars, Zane rose and paced the floor. Remembering Beth and Hannah and the bigger picture and making an effort to sound cheerful, he hoped the forced enthusiasm didn't come across as fake as Valerie's. "*Things* are coming along fine. Still working out some details, but moving in the right direction."

Not yet.

"They're at an impasse, folks." Valerie sounded thrilled at the prospect.

Zane suppressed the denial that sprang to his lips. He had a bigger problem to work on than Valerie Simons' determined exploitation.

"You'll let us know the minute you seal the deal?"

Imagining her look of mock innuendo at the audience, Zane ground out, "You'll be the first to know."

Not. He tossed the cell on the couch; took a restless turn around the room ending up in front of the bay of windows, hands shoved in his pockets. He didn't see the parade of cars going by below, instead he heard Lacey's voice in his head.

Let's be honest here—

Yes, let's.

She wasn't wrong. For him their contest *had* started

out as a science experiment. But somewhere along the way, it'd turned into something else.

Of course he'd blown it. Big time. Pushed the best thing to ever happen to him away because he— He was afraid the love he felt for Lacey wouldn't last. Hadn't his mother proven there was no possible way it could?

Zane scowled at the refurbished warehouse across the street. Lacey wasn't wrong. There was no rule that said he couldn't rewrite the game plan. As a scientist, he knew how to observe, make objective assessments, then draw up a plan of action based on those conclusions. From experience he knew, sometimes an experiment gone wrong needed new parameters. A revision of its paradigm and baseline algorithm.

With a little tweaking, if the stars aligned, and he was lucky, and if he took a page out of Lacey's book, it was possible to get an outcome he could live with...for the rest of his life.

By Sunday afternoon Lacey was sick of her own company. Beth and Hannah were spending the day at the Oregon Museum of Science and Industry. Zane had abruptly stopped leaving messages. Not that she wanted to talk to him. Still, the quiet settling in her apartment had a lonely component that was new and chilling.

Wasn't that what she wanted? For Zane Tyler to go away and leave her alone?

If that was the case, why was she watching the show when Valerie Simons made the call to Zane on Friday? And why did the sound of his too-cheerful voice— it seemed to her—and confident conclusion have her biting her nails through the whole segment?

Ever since, her mind churned through every moment she'd spent with the impossible man. She couldn't let go of what could be, if only they'd given it a chance.

Her decision to abandon the impossible man and their so called contest wavered. She'd known what she was getting into when she dragged Zane to his bedroom. It wasn't his fault she'd blown right through all the stop signs.

Marching into the kitchen to load the dishwasher, she brushed the moisture gathering in her eyes with the back of one hand. How she'd felt about her ex was nothing compared to the hurt and anger and...yes... love for Zane storming through her. She was in big trouble. Getting over Stephen had not been easy, but she'd managed. In comparison, getting over Zane, she was afraid, would take a lifetime.

You made a mistake. Get over it, girl.

It didn't take long to clean up the few dishes in her sink. Ignoring the half-done panes of Georgette and the Professor's next encounter waiting to be finished, she sank into a chair at the table, fingering the gilded invitation she'd been avoiding all weekend.

The Turning-Thirty Reunion was two weeks away. She'd wanted a date for the event; even had half-considered asking Zane until everything blew up Friday. But, more shocking than asking the Professor if he would accompany her, was how much she wanted more than a simple date, or to win Valerie's stupid contest. She wanted Zane with her whole heart, plain and simple.

The chocolates, the way he offered her a seat not knowing how weak in the knees she got at the smile turning up the corners of his lips when he found a situation amusing; how he'd rested his hand protectively on the small of her back as they'd walked the few blocks to his place. All of that had shown her a side to the Professor he kept hidden with all his talk of science being the ruling factor in a woman falling for a guy.

The truth was, she hardly knew Zane Tyler. Except she felt like she'd known him forever.

If he ever fell in love, she knew in her heart, he'd never let his girl down. He was the perfect guy, for her, Lacey Daniels. Not because he smelled fantastic, which he did, but because he was everything she'd ever hoped to find. No matter how much he frustrated her or she thought his outlandish ideas on the questionable side, all she wanted was to wake up beside Zane for the rest of her life.

The man loves his fragrances, so turn the tables on him.

"Ge, you're a genius!" Jumping to her feet, Lacey went to her bedroom. On her vanity were half a dozen perfumes she rarely wore. She knew which one to pick. Spraying Pikake into the air, she walked through the flowery scented mist.

There was more than one way to skin a cat and this one had a thing for exotic smells.

Could they make a deal? For forever?

Her cell rang. She recognized the number. "Hi. I was just about to call."

"Good." The rough rasp of Zane's voice sent a happy, dancing shiver down her spine. "But let me go first."

Lacey's heart gave a hopeful skip. "Okay."

"Have you read this morning's *Oregon Tribune*?"

"Haven't had a chance."

Not a complete fib. She had been busy trying to figure out what to do about the man who made her body melt every time she thought of exploring that big bed of his again.

"Check out the front page of the *Living Today* section."

Going to the table, Lacey flipped open the paper. A headline jumped out.

How To Use Pheromones AND Romance To Find The Perfect Mate.

She skimmed the article and laughed, "Nicely done, Professor. Where are you?"

"Look out your window."

Lacey pulled the drapes aside. Zane stood on the sidewalk holding a dozen crimson roses. Behind him a jazz band played. "I have a new challenge for you, Lacey Daniels."

"Stay there. Don't move." She tossed the cell on her desk and was out the door, down the steps, and throwing herself at the man who'd given her the one thing she'd never thought she needed. A scientist.

"Mmmm." He buried his nose in her neck.

He was perfect and everything she (and Ge) wanted.

Heart filling, Lacey took the biggest leap of all. "Thought you'd like the smell. Does it make you dream of that one special girl?"

"You're that girl. For me." He whispered against her lips, "Marry me. Be my wife?"

Trust and a lifetime commitment wouldn't always be easy, but with Zane they'd conquer the hurdles together. Raining kisses on his face, there was just one answer she could give. "Yes, Professor, I would be honored to marry you!"

AUTHOR BIO

Like all children of military families, Susan spent her childhood moving from one duty station to the next. An ardent student of human nature, she acquired a love for ancient history and myth, a fascination for the ridiculous and unusual, and is the first to admit, she still collects way too much useless information. These days, when not working as a Registered Nurse, she writes whenever she can. When not writing, her favorite things to do are spend time with family, read, watch movies, garden, take black-and-white photos, travel, and remodel her house.

Website: www.susanlute.com/

Instagram: authorsusanlute

Pinterest: www.pinterest.com/sidella/

Facebook: www.facebook.com/pages/Susan-Lute/202040233153546

Goodreads: www.goodreads.com/author/show/1252907.Susan_Lute

Twitter: www.twitter.com/SusanLute

THANK YOU!

THANK YOU FOR READING LOVE Lessons. I hope you enjoyed how Lacey and Zane found love in the most unlikely place. If you did, and you have a moment to help other readers find this book, please leave a review at the retailer where you bought your copy. And, if you could recommend it to friends, on the reader sites you visit, and on social media, that would be so helpful in building love for this book and the ones that follow.

If you're like me, you live a very busy life, and may have little time to follow authors whose stories speak to you. Want an update on new releases? Try a short story for FREE and sign up for my newsletter at *https://bit.ly/2nPkEVY* to receive an occasional email about upcoming events and the books I write.

Thank you for being a reader!

OTHER BOOKS IN THE
SELLWOOD NOVELLA SERIES

OTHER BOOKS BY
SUSAN LUTE

The Girl Most Likely To: An Anthology
The Gift Of Christmas: An Anthology
Gifts From The Heart: An Anthology

Oops...We're Married? A Silhouette Romance
Classic

Read on for a sneak preview of

A FOOL FOR LOVE ~
A SELLWOOD NOVELLA,
BOOK ONE

WHEN THE ENGINE COUGHED, ALICE York swore softly under her breath. Not at her beloved '55 Ford pickup – a classic she'd restored right down to the high-gloss, apple-green paint – but at the timing. The middle of rush hour traffic in Sellwood, a bohemian suburb of Portland, was not the place for the Ford's pampered engine to have a coughing fit.

"Just like a man," she muttered. "Flaking out right when a girl needs him the most. Hadn't expected that from the greatest cowboy in history."

Muscling the ton and a half, solid truck with its caravan-style canopy onto a tree-lined side street, Alice sighed in relief when they made it halfway down the block before Duke sputtered to a stop at the curb in front of an elegant, gray Victorian house. An elaborately carved sign read, Martha's Elder House.

She slumped in the seat and closed her eyes. She had to get to Dave's Classic Restorations, fifty-five miles away in Longview, where a job working on old classics like Duke waited. With exactly one hundred, twenty-seven dollars and fifty-one cents in her purse, she had barely enough to rent a room and stave off hunger until her first paycheck.

Working on classic cars was good work when she

could get it, putting enough money in her pocket so she could make it to her next destination, wherever that might be. And if she was lucky, along the stretch of road ahead of her, she could usually get in a painting or two.

But having to shell out a chunk of her scant reserves for new parts, plus take time to fix the Ford?

She banged her head gently on the steering wheel. She'd had one rule from the very first day she'd taken to the road. A litany of poor-me was not allowed in Duke's cab. Melting into a puddle of panic was not an option.

Hood raised, her head, arms, and shoulders buried in the engine compartment, she tested connections. A door banged behind her with the force of furious anger.

A man's raised voice demanded, "Where are you going?"

Surprised, Alice jerked, hit her head on the hood, and saw stars. "Holy mother of—"

"You don't pay me enough to put up with that old man's insults!" A woman shouted, the voice shrill, pampered. Stilettos clattered past Alice.

Sneakers thumping the sidewalk followed, appearing briefly in her peripheral vision as she rubbed her scalp while blinking back waterworks.

Heavier boots stopped beside the truck. "You can't be serious, Penelope. He's not saying you're a horrible cook. He just likes pushing your buttons."

All Alice could see were denim-clad legs — strong, masculine legs that would make any woman worth her salt salivate.

What now? Make her presence known? Or pretend she wasn't a witness to this very public domestic squabble.

Staccato beeps released a car lock again and again and again. Two car doors slammed, a high-octane engine roared to life, tires squealed, and the decision was taken out of her hands.

"Lady," the masculine voice sharp with anger now, addressed her. "You can't park that monstrosity here."

Insulted beyond belief, Alice banged her head again and came out fighting. "The Duke is not a monstrosity!"

Dark brows knitted together, lips stretched in a straight line, the man belonging to the heart-thumping man-legs raised his snapping gaze from her backside to her face.

A flash fire of smothering heat burned from said bottom to her cheeks. *Holy mama!*

Her outraged drained while all her girly parts awoke with a shout. *Hello!*

His short, dark hair was painted by the sun with bold blonde streaks. Stormy blue eyes cut her no slack. The unshaven stubble covering a stubborn chin gave him a sexy look that would be hard for any woman to ignore. Alice was nothing but appreciative.

Faced with a long neglected libido gone wild, she cocked one hip. Folding her arms across her chest, the temptation to trace the line of that stubborn jaw with fingers that itched to explore was hard to fight.

Glaring Sexy Guy probably wouldn't appreciate the grease she'd leave behind, unless he like his casual associations slick and dirty.

"You have to move it." His tone erased any humor her last thought inspired.

His glare didn't intimidate her. She'd seen worse. "Can't."

He matched her stance. "Why?"

"Not going anywhere until I get a new fuel pump."

His glower deepened.

"Dad!" A young girl bounced down the front porch steps, interrupting whatever demand Sexy Guy was about to make. Blonde hair, trapped in ponytails, bounced. "Is Penelope gone?"

"Yes." He noticeably tugged on the reins of his temper for the sake of the child.

Alice gave him a point for good behavior.

"Did she take that creep Blake with her?"

His head snapped toward the girl. It was easy to follow his thoughts.

A sour taste sprang up in Alice's mouth. Had this Blake fellow been a creep to the blue-eyed child with the innocent face?

"Lucy, did Blake—"

The girl shuddered. "Ewe, Dad. No!"

Sexy Guy's shoulders relaxed. Mentally Alice chalked a second point in his column.

He drew a deep breath. "Yes they're both gone."

The girl pumped her fist, then turned to stare at Duke. "Wow. Cool color."

Her hand, lured by the enticing, shiny apple-green paint, stretched to stroke the truck.

Alice leaned forward to see if the kid had noticed the road winding through city scape she'd painted last month on the length of that side of the truck.

She raised an eyebrow. Lucy cocked her head. "Is this truck yours?"

Sexy Guy placed a protective hand on his daughter's slight shoulder. "Luce, watch your manners."

The man making her heart beat like it was in the middle of an Olympic triathlon was a dad. Probably had a wife. That might have been the little woman who'd just made her temperamental exit.

As for his daughter, the girl was precocious and spoke her mind. Alice liked that in a person, whether man or child. But Lucy wasn't the only one who could be direct. "Yes, it is. And who might you be?"

"Lucy. I'm twelve." Sharp chin elevating, reminded Alice what it was like to be young and having to face unexpected, crushing changes. The kid tilted her head toward Sexy Guy. "That's Zach, my dad."

Doing her best to ignore frowning Sexy Dad, Alice stretched out a hand to Lucy. "Nice to meet you. I'm Alice York."

Very adult-like, Lucy met her halfway, pumped once, let go and grinned.

Alice's chest swelled with the feeling of having hit a home run. Quickly she stepped back. Making friends was okay. Getting attached to the girl's spunk wasn't.

An older man, with a striking resemblance to Zach, ambled down the porch steps to join them. He circled Duke with a low whistle before stopping next to Alice. "This your rig, young lady?"

She grinned. Young was a relative term. Some days like today, twenty-six didn't feel as young it should. "Yes."

After introductions, he ogled Duke and the over-the-top gypsy-colored canopy nestled in the bed. When he was done, twinkling blue eyes fastened on Alice. "Beautiful. Just beautiful."

She swallowed sudden laughter. The older version of Zach had a lot more charm than his more youthful relative.

Lucy leaned into old guy's arm. "Papa, Penelope and Blake are gone."

"Good riddance is all I have to say."

Zach rolled his eyes. "Granddad, I'm trying to teach her manners."

"And a good father you are, too." Granddad slapped Zach on the back. "Those two where freeloaders. I'm not sorry to see them go."

"You're impossible. You know that, right?" The fight had gone out of Zach's tone, replaced by laughter threatening to pull his fascinating mouth into a crooked smile.

Sexy Guy clearly loved his grandfather. Grudgingly she gave him another point. But just because he was racking up good-guy points didn't mean she could jump his bones the first chance she got, even though that was exactly the insane image floating through her surprisingly alert mind.

Stop staring, Alice ordered her out of control libido.

Sudden desire took a nosedive when he turned a stern eye in her direction. "You'll have to call a tow truck and get that—" eyes narrowed, he gestured rudely at Duke. "—moved as soon as possible. This is a no-parking zone."

Alice's hackles stood up to be counted. "We won't be here long if I can find a store that carries the part."

Zach's granddad rubbed his chin. "That truck's a classic. Won't be easy to find parts on a Friday night. And a holiday weekend to boot."

Frustration matching Zach Barret's replaced the temper she'd been holding with a tight reign. Broke down in a no-park zone in Sellwood, with no way to lay her hands on the part she needed, put a serious knot in the time line she'd allotted to get to the new job. No job meant no money. No money meant being stuck. And unlike these nice strangers in their nice house, getting stuck in one place was the last thing she would let happen again.

RT Book Reviews ~ *"A delightful, fast-moving romance that restores any loss of belief in the saying 'Who has loved that loved not at first sight?' The two main characters are fully formed and the secondary characters give this novella the substance of a full-length novel."*

Susan Lute is a beautiful keeper of the human heart. She explores the soul and leaves the reader certain life is worth the journey. ~ Wendy Warren, 2-time recipient of the prestigious RITA Award

www.ingramcontent.com/pod-product-compliance
Lightning Source LLC
Chambersburg PA
CBHW051922220626
47052CB00003B/543